NEW YORK REVIEW BOOKS
CLASSICS

T0017677

MY DEATH

LISA TUTTLE was born and raised in Houston, Texas, and moved to Britain in the 1980s. Her first book, *Windhaven* (1981), cowritten with George R. R. Martin, was followed by more than three dozen fantasy, science-fiction, mystery, and horror novels written for both adults and children, and her widely anthologized short stories have been collected into several volumes, including *A Nest of Nightmares*, *The Dead Hours of the Night*, and *Riding the Nightmare*. Since receiving the John W. Campbell Award for Best New Writer in 1974, Tuttle has been nominated and short-listed for many major science-fiction prizes, winning a British Science Fiction Award in 1990 and an International Horror Guild Award in 2008. She is the author of *The Encyclopedia of Feminism* and currently writes a monthly science-fiction review column for *The Guardian*. She lives with her husband and their daughter in Scotland.

AMY GENTRY is the author of the novels *Good As Gone*, *Last Woman Standing*, and, most recently, *Bad Habits*. Her essays, reviews, and profiles have appeared in the *Chicago Tribune*, *Salon*, *The Paris Review*, and *Texas Monthly*. She holds a doctorate in English from the University of Chicago and lives in Austin, Texas.

MY DEATH

LISA TUTTLE

Introduction by
AMY GENTRY

NEW YORK REVIEW BOOKS

New York

THIS IS A NEW YORK REVIEW BOOK
PUBLISHED BY THE NEW YORK REVIEW OF BOOKS
207 East 32nd Street, New York, NY 10016
www.nyrb.com

First published as a New York Review Books Classic in 2023.

Library of Congress Cataloging-in-Publication Data
Names: Tuttle, Lisa, 1952– author. | Gentry, Amy, writer of introduction.
Title: My death / by Lisa Tuttle; introduction by Amy Gentry.
Description: New York: New York Review Books, 2023. | Series: New York
    Review Books Classics
Identifiers: LCCN 2023000790 (print) | LCCN 2023000791 (ebook) |
    ISBN 9781681377728 (paperback) | ISBN 9781681377735 (ebook)
Subjects: LCGFT: Novellas.
Classification: LCC PS3570.U85 M967 2023 (print) | LCC PS3570.U85 (ebook) |
    DDC 813/.54—dc23/eng/20230109
LC record available at https://lccn.loc.gov/2023000790
LC ebook record available at https://lccn.loc.gov/2023000791

ISBN 978-1-68137-772-8
Available as an electronic book; ISBN 978-1-68137-773-5

Printed in the United States of America on acid-free paper.
10 9 8 7 6 5 4 3 2 1

INTRODUCTION

There's something about a book you find by accident, a book no one else seems to have heard of, a book that thrills and then becomes a part of you, when it's one you so easily might never have read at all—it seems like it found you.

—Lisa Tuttle, "The Book That Finds You"

WHY DO we long to know more about the lives of our most treasured authors? They're just people with cavities and grocery lists, like the rest of us. Perhaps what we really crave isn't knowledge of them but of the selves their words conjured when we first encountered them in an armchair or subway car or childhood home, a mental topography now haunted by that initial meeting between author and reader. The subgenre that exists to satisfy this curiosity—the "romance of the archive," exemplified by A. S. Byatt's *Possession*—freely acknowledges the complications of such an entanglement. But Lisa Tuttle's novella *My Death* goes further, warning against the self-knowledge gained by venturing too far into that uncanny landscape.

The opening pages of *My Death* seem to promise nothing more than a cozy tale of literary detective work. The narrator, who remains unnamed throughout the story, is a recently widowed novelist living on Scotland's craggy western shore, her career stalled out by grief. While visiting the National Gallery in Edinburgh, she comes upon a portrait of the painter and writer Helen Ralston, an early-twentieth-century visionary whose work has long been overshadowed by her tempestuous affair with a more famous male author, W. E. Logan. Having been heavily influenced by Ralston's work as a young woman, the narrator embarks on a biography that will elevate her from muse to "forgotten modernist"—and, it is implied, help the narrator rediscover the wellspring of her own creativity.

The investigation begins auspiciously enough. Helen Ralston is not only still alive at ninety-four but lucid, free of troublesome heirs, and eager to hand over her cache of journals and letters to the narrator. When the narrator gains access to a rare Ralston painting, however, a creeping sense of unease begins to steal into the text. Reality ripples and warps around the artwork; she looks at her trusted agent, who introduced her to its owner, and feels only "a clutch of fear, because I was a woman, and my only way out was blocked by two men." It's as if something has entered the text and wrenched it out of her hands—not quite gender itself, but some savage specter of gender.

The moment passes, but reality never quite recovers. As the biographer draws closer to her subject, the uncanny lingers like a scent. Dreams and coincidences take on a sinister cast. We are reminded that every biography ends in death, and the impossibility of the title—its elliptical, unresolved circularity—begins to infect the narrative. By the time we are caught in its trap, it's too late.

Like both Ralston and the narrator of *My Death*, Tuttle is an American expat. Born in 1952 in Houston, Texas, she first traveled to England in 1980, eventually taking up permanent residence in Torinturk, Scotland, where she lives with her husband, the writer and editor Colin Murray. Her long residence in the United Kingdom, and the lack of availability of much of her output in the United States, might explain why she's not as widely known in her native country as she should be. But in the science-fiction, fantasy, and horror worlds, her name has been a byword for smart, psychologically grounded, award-winning speculative fiction for forty years. Before Valancourt Press's recent reissue of her 1986 story collection, *A Nest of Nightmares*, paperback copies sold for several hundred dollars apiece online. She is a horror writer's horror writer.

Tuttle began writing early—"before I could read," she says—and later started typing her stories on an old typewriter her father gave her when she was nine years old. From her father, too, came her earliest exposure to "weird tales"; one early photograph shows a two-year-old Tuttle lying on her parents' bed, pretending to read a science-fiction magazine. By high school, she had discovered the fan clubs advertised in the backs of those magazines—sci-fi, fantasy, and horror were all classed together, well outside the mainstream—and begun corresponding by mail with authors and fans around the world. In a testament to how small and tight-knit the community was at the time, the fan club she founded as a high schooler once hosted the well-known speculative-fiction writer Harlan Ellison at a meeting in her parents' living room. She did not tell him she wrote her own stories, reluctant to put herself on the same footing as a published author but feeling the word "aspiring" didn't do justice to her seriousness. Years later, they met again at the Clarion Science Fiction and Fantasy Writers' Workshop and he became her mentor in earnest. At that point, she was a student at

Syracuse University, which she had chosen to attend in part because she already knew science-fiction fans there; one of her advisers had formerly advised Joyce Carol Oates, whose macabre stories she admired. Ignoring Ellison's characteristically blunt advice to drop out of college and "just write!" she nevertheless graduated early, in three years.

After a brief stint house-sitting for Ellison in Los Angeles after college, she moved to Austin, Texas, where she worked for the *Austin American-Statesman*, starting as a typist hired to computerize the paper's archive and rising through the ranks to become the paper's first TV critic. Austin, already a booming university town, was becoming a hub for science-fiction writers. In 1973, one of Tuttle's friends dubbed their unofficial gatherings the "Turkey City Writer's Workshop and Neo-Pro Rodeo," and over the years the workshop (which still exists, having dropped the rodeo part) hosted a parade of now-venerable science-fiction authors. During that time, Tuttle met and briefly dated George R. R. Martin, coauthoring a series of short stories with him that were later published as the novel *Windhaven* (1981).

She also met her first husband, the British writer Christopher Priest. In 1980, Tuttle moved to England and married Priest "in pursuit of a romantic dream" that soon fell apart, an experience she would later plumb with a wild, willful intensity in her novel *The Pillow Friend* (1996). But by then, her career was beginning to take off. She chose to stay in London, publishing her first two solo novels, *Familiar Spirit* (1983) and *Gabriel* (1987), shortly afterward. *Nest of Nightmares* and two additional collections, *A Spaceship Built of Stone* (1987) and *Memories of the Body* (1990), followed, along with an ambitious *Encyclopedia of Feminism* (1986) and various children's books and side projects, some written under pen names. Tuttle's output has remained steady ever since, forming an impressive and frequently anthologized back catalog of dark fantasy, folk horror, body horror, science fiction, and even erotica, most written from the point of view of women. *My Death*, first published in the United Kingdom by PS Publishing in 2004, and later in a small edition in the United States by the feminist science-fiction house Aqueduct Press, marks almost the exact midpoint of her career.

Though Tuttle does not hesitate to call herself a feminist—her encyclopedia holds up surprisingly well—her predominant trait as a storyteller is not her allegiance to any one ideology but rather a probing curiosity about women's experience. Like her spiritual godmother Shirley Jackson, she works mainly in a form of grounded psychological horror that Tuttle describes as "a kind of realism where something other breaks through." But Tuttle's heroines have forsaken Jackson's domestic spaces to navigate the double and triple binds of post-second-wave womanhood, ping-ponging between satisfaction and regret, self-sufficiency and loneliness. As in Henry James's ghost stories, hauntings, possessions, time loops, and doppelgängers follow with a perverse logic from these contradictions; monsters and ancient curses are not necessary to explain the eruption of the supernatural into our world. Unspeakable desire is enough.

Tuttle was inspired to write *My Death* after reading Deborah Baker's 1994 biography of the eccentric American avant-garde poet Laura Riding. Though Tuttle freely mixed in details from the biographies of other modernists, many incidents in *My Death* are drawn directly from Riding's life, including her expatriation from America to Europe, a presumed suicide attempt from a window during an argument with then-lover Robert Graves and his wife, and her role as the unwitting "muse" for Graves's mythopoeic book of poetry scholarship, *The White Goddess*. According to an anecdote Tuttle once read, when Graves and Riding first saw the island of Majorca, where they would live together for six years, Riding cried, "I have seen my death!"—a quote Tuttle confesses she "may have dreamed," since she hasn't been able to find it since. (Neither have I.) In any case, it was Graves, not Riding, who eventually died on Majorca. Perhaps Riding, whom contemporaries frequently vilified as a witch, sensed a more spiritual death coming; her memoir accuses Graves of stealing and distorting material she came up with when they lived together on the island.

My Death does not touch on Riding's esoteric theories about male-female relations, or on her lifelong fury over Graves's alleged theft. Yet *My Death* picks compulsively at the issue of the erasure of women's authorship by men. Along with *The Pillow Friend*, a novel about the psychosexual fantasies of a woman writer who moves to England to be with a famous poet, and "The Book That Finds You" (2015), a story that draws on the fraught relationship between writers Robert Aickman and Elizabeth Jane Howard, *My Death* forms something of a trilogy about existing as a woman writer in the company of men. Given all this, it would be easy to read into *My Death* a certain ambivalence on Tuttle's part about her own close relationships with authors in her genre like Martin and Priest. The science-fiction scene that nurtured and supported Tuttle's talent was still overwhelmingly dominated by men, despite game-changing contributions by pioneering writers like Joanna Russ, Octavia Butler,

Connie Willis, and Ursula K. Le Guin. Tuttle's protagonists are, if not exactly oppressed by men, at least hemmed in on all sides; like the narrator of *My Death*, they might at any moment look around and realize the exit is blocked.

But despite its clear investment in feminist recovery projects, *My Death*'s romantic relationship is ultimately, like Ralston's painting, a kind of trompe l'oeil. As a character, poor Willy Logan proves barely more substantial than the body part to which his name comically alludes. The novella's central relationship is the one between the narrator and the elderly Ralston, a vision of herself as seen in a trick mirror. The desire the narrator feels, shared by all of Tuttle's women artists, is ultimately not the desire for a lover, a child, a name, or even a career, but for a self, always lost, perhaps just around the corner, if you only knew where to look. It is the self, not the man, that tantalizes and entraps. Tuttle's characters always take the bait.

We are long overdue for a Lisa Tuttle renaissance. Her piercing investigations of gender and bodily autonomy, her crossings and migrations and eternal returns, and her sly, unsettling, everyday terrors have never felt more relevant. The question is not if but when her books will find you. And when they do, who knows what they will do with you?

—AMY GENTRY

MY DEATH

why must I write?
you would not care for this,
but She draws the veil aside,

unbinds my eyes,
commands,
write, write or die.
                    —H.D., *Hermetic Definition*

...a typical death island where the familiar Death-goddess
sings as she spins.
                    —ROBERT GRAVES, *The Greek Myths*

As i travelled, I watched the landscape—lochs and hillsides, the trees still winter-bare, etched against a soft, grey sky—and all the time my empty hand moved on my lap, tracing the pattern the branches made, smoothing the lines of the hills.

That drawing could be a way of not thinking and a barrier against feeling I didn't need a psychotherapist to tell me. Once upon a time I would have whiled away the journey by making up stories, but since Allan's death, this escape had failed me.

I had been a writer all my life—professionally, thirty years—but the urge to make up stories went back even further. Whether they were for my own private entertainment or printed out and hand-bound as presents for family, whether they appeared in fanzines or between hardcovers, one thousand words long or one hundred thousand, sold barely two hundred copies or hovered at the bottom of (one) best-seller list, whether they won glowing reviews or were uniformly ignored, my stories were me, they were what I did. Publishers might fail me, readers lose interest, but that story itself let me down was something that had never occurred before.

Strange that I could still take pleasure in sketching, because that was so completely associated with my life with Allan that the reminder ought to have been too painful. He had been a keen amateur artist, a weekend watercolorist, and, following his relaxed example, I'd tried my hand on our first holiday together and liked the results. It became something we could do together, another shared interest. I had not painted or sketched since childhood, having decided very early in life that I must devote myself to the one thing I was good at in order to succeed. Anything else seemed like a waste of time.

Allan had never seen life in those terms; he came from a different world. He was English, middle-class, ten years older than me. My parents were self-made, first-generation Americans who knew and thought little about what their parents had left behind, whereas his could trace their ancestry back to the Middle Ages, and while they were nothing so vulgar as rich, they had never had to worry about money. Allan had gone to a "progressive" school where the importance of being well-rounded was emphasized and little attention given to the practicalities of earning a living. And so he was athletic—he could play cricket and football, swim, shoot, and sail—and musical, and artistic, and handy—a good plain cook, he could put up a garden shed or any large item of flat-packed furniture by himself—and prodigiously well-read. But, as he sometimes said with a sigh, his skills were many, useful, and entertaining, but not the sort to attract financial reward.

We'd been living modestly but comfortably mainly on his investments, augmented by my erratic writing income, until the collapse of the stock-market. Before we'd done more than consider ways we might live even more modestly, Allan had died from a massive heart attack.

I had no debts—even the mortgage was paid off—but my writing income had dried to the merest trickle, and the past year and a half had eaten away at my savings. Something had to change—which was why I was on my way to Edinburgh to meet my agent.

I hadn't seen Selwyn in several years. At least, not on business—he had come up to Scotland for Allan's funeral. When he'd sent me an email to say he would be in Edinburgh on business, and was it possible I'd be free for lunch, I'd known it was an opportunity I had to take. I'd written nothing to speak of since Allan's death, one year and five months ago. I still didn't know if I would ever want to write again, but I had to make some money, and I wasn't trained or qualified to do anything else. The prospect of embarking, in my fifties, on a new, low-paid career as a cleaner or carer was too grim to contemplate.

I'd hoped having a deadline would focus my mind, but by the time I arrived at Waverley Station the only thing I felt sure of was that, as stories had failed me, my next book would have to be nonfiction.

I arrived with time to spare and, as it wasn't raining and was, for February, remarkably mild, I took a stroll up to the National Gallery. Access to art was one thing I really missed in my remote country home. I had lots of books, but reproductions just weren't the same as being able to wander around a spacious gallery staring at the original paintings.

It was hard to relax and concentrate on the pictures that day; my mind was jittering around, desperate for an idea. And then all of a sudden, there *she* was.

I knew her, standing there, an imposing female figure in a dark purple robe, crowned with a gold filigreed tiara in her reddish-gold hair, one slim white arm held up commandingly, her pale face stern and angular, not entirely beautiful, but unique, arresting, and as intimately familiar to me as were the fleshy, naked-looking pink and grey swine who scattered and bolted in terror before her. I also knew the pile of stones behind her, and the grove of trees, and, in the middle distance, the sly, crouching figure of her nemesis hiding behind a rock as he watched and waited.

Circe, 1928, by W. E. Logan.

It was like coming across an old friend in an unfamiliar place. As a college student, I'd had a poster-print of this same painting hanging on the wall of my dormitory room. Later, it had accompanied me to adorn various apartments in New York, Seattle, New Orleans, and Austin, but, despite my affection for it, I'd never bothered to have it framed, and by the time I left for London it was too frayed and torn and stained to move again.

For ten eventful, formative years this picture had been part of my life. I had gazed up at her, and Circe had looked down on me through times of heart-break and exultation, in boredom and in ecstasy. I much preferred the powerful enchantress who would turn men into pigs to the dreamier, more passive maidens beloved of my contemporaries. The walls of my friends' rooms featured reproductions of Pre-Raphaelite beauties: poor, drowned Ophelia, Mariana waiting patiently at her window, Isabella moping over her pot of basil. I preferred Circe's more angular and determined features, her lively, impatient stare: *Cast out that swine!* she advised. *All men are pigs. You don't need them. Live alone, like me, and make magic.*

I gazed with wonder at the original painting. It was so much more vivid and alive than the rather dull tones of the reproduction. Although I'd visited the Scottish National

Gallery many times, I could not remember having seen it here before. Now I noticed details in it that I didn't recall from the reproduction: the distinct shape of oak-leaf, and a scattering of acorns on the ground; a line of alders in the distance—alders, the tree of resurrection and concealment—and above, in a patch of blue sky, hovered a tiny bird, Circe's namesake, the female falcon.

My fascination with this painting when I was younger was mostly to do with the subject matter: I liked pictures that told a story, and the stories I liked best were from ancient mythology. I had been sadly disappointed by all the other paintings by W. E. Logan that I had managed to track down: they were either landscapes (mostly of the South of France) or dull portraits of middle-class Glaswegians.

Circe, which marked a total departure in style and approach, had also been W. E. Logan's last completed painting. His model was a young art student called Helen Elizabeth Ralston—an American who had gone to Glasgow to study art. Shortly after Logan completed his study of her as the enchantress, she had fallen—or leaped—from the high window of a flat in the west end of Glasgow. Although badly injured, she survived. Logan had left his wife and children to devote himself to Helen. He paid for her operations and the medical care she needed, and during the long hours he spent sitting at her bedside, he'd made up a story about a little girl who had walked out of a high window and discovered a world of adventure in the clouds high above the city. As he talked, he sketched, creating a sharp-nosed determined little girl menaced and befriended by weird, amorphous cloud-shapes, and then he put the pictures in order, and wrote up the text to create *Hermine in Cloud-Land*, his first book and a popular seller in Britain throughout the 1930s.

The real Helen Ralston was not only Logan's muse and inspiration, but went on to become a successful writer herself. She'd written the cult classic *In Troy*, that amazing, poetic cry of a book, which throughout my twenties had been practically my Bible.

And yet I'd had no idea, when I'd huddled on my bed and lost myself in the mythic story and compelling, almost ritualistic phrases of *In Troy*, that its author was staring down at me from the wall. I'd only discovered that in the early 1980s, when I was living in London and *In Troy* was reprinted as one of those green-backed Virago Classics, with a detail from W. E. Logan's *Circe* on the cover. Angela Carter had written the appreciative introduction to the reprint, and it was there that I had learned of Helen Elizabeth Ralston's relationship with W. E. (Willy) Logan.

Feeling suddenly much livelier, I left the gallery and went down Princes Street to the big bookshop there. I couldn't find *In Troy* or anything else by Helen Ralston in the fiction section. Browsing through the essays and criticism I eventually found a book called *A Late Flowering* by some American academic, which devoted a chapter to the books of Helen Ralston. Willy Logan was better represented. Under "L" in the fiction section was a whole row of his novels, the uniform edition from Canongate. The only book I'd read of his was one based on Celtic mythology, which had been published, with an amazing George Barr cover, in the Ballantine Adult Fantasy line around about 1968. I remembered nothing at all about it now, not even the title.

After a little hesitation I decided to try *In Circe's Snare* for its suggestive title, and I also bought *Second Chance at Life* by Brian Ross, a big fat biography of Logan, recently published. And then I noticed the time and knew I had to run.

SELWYN was waiting for me at the restaurant. He stood up, beaming, and came over to give me a close, warm hug.

"My dear. You're looking very well."

I'd been feeling flushed and sweaty, but his appreciative gaze made me feel better. He'd always had the knack of that. Selwyn was an attractive man, even if these days he had to rely on expensive, well-cut clothes to disguise his expanding middle. His hair, no longer long and shaggy, nevertheless was still thick and only slightly sprinkled with grey. When young, he'd worn little round Lennon-type glasses; now, contact lenses made his brown eyes even more liquid, and his eyelashes were as enviably thick and black as I remembered.

"Let's order quickly, and then we can talk," he said after I was settled. "I've already ordered wine, if white's all right with you; if not—"

"It's fine. What do you recommend?"

"Everything is good here; the crab cakes are sensational."

"That sounds good." I was relieved not to have to bother with the menu, being a little out of practice with restaurants. "Crab cakes with a green salad."

Smoothly he summoned the waiter and swiftly sent him away again, and then those brown eyes, gentle yet disconcertingly sharp, were focused on me again. "So. How *are* you? Really."

"Fine. I'm fine. I mean—I'm not, not really, but, you know, life goes on. I'm OK."

"Writing again?"

I took a deep breath and shook my head.

His eyebrows went up. "But—your novel. You were writing a novel."

He meant a year and a half ago.

"It wasn't any good."

"Please. You're much too close to it. You need another perspective. Send it to me, whatever you've got, and I'll give you my thoughts on it. I'll be honest, I promise."

I trusted Selwyn's opinion more than most, but I'd never liked anyone reading my rough drafts—sometimes I could scarcely bear to read them through myself. This one was permeated by Allan, and the happy, hopeful person who had written it was gone.

"There's no point," I said. "I'm not going to finish it. Even if you liked it, even if there's something good in it—too much has changed. I can't get back into that frame of mind; I don't even want to try. I need to get on and write the *next* book."

"All right. That sounds good to me. So what might the next book be?"

To my relief, the waiter arrived with our drinks. When the wine had been poured, I raised my glass to his and said, "To the next book!"

"To the next book," he agreed. We clinked glasses and sipped, and then he waited for me to explain.

Finally I said, "It's going to be nonfiction."

My last nonfiction book had been published nearly fifteen years ago and had been neither a howling success nor a disaster. There had been good reviews, and the first printing had sold out. Unfortunately for me, there was never a second printing, nor the expected paperback sale. The publisher was taken over in mid-process, and my editor was among the many staff members to be "rationalized" and let go. My book got lost in the shuffle, and by the time I'd come up with an idea for another, the fashion had changed, no one was really interested, and my brave new career as an author of popular nonfiction had fizzled out. All that was a very long time ago: I didn't see why I shouldn't be allowed to start again.

Selwyn nodded. When he spoke, I could tell that his thoughts had been following the same track as mine. "It was the publisher's fault that you didn't do a lot better last time. That was a good book, and it always had the potential to be a steady seller on the back-list. I don't know why they didn't stick with it, but it was nothing to do with you—you did a great job with it, and it could have, *should* have, launched a whole new career for you." He paused to take a drink of wine and then looked at me inquiringly. "What sort of nonfiction?"

"Biography?"

"Perfect. With your understanding of characters, your ability to bring them to life in fiction—yes, you'd do very well, writing a life."

Even though I knew it was his job to build me up and promote me, I couldn't help feeling pleased. I responded to his praise like a parched plant to water.

"Really?"

"Absolutely." He beamed. "There's always a demand for good biographies, so selling it shouldn't be tough. I don't know how much I could get you up-front, that would depend—they can be expensive projects, you know, take a long time to write, and there's travel, research . . . of course, there are grants, too—" he broke off suddenly and cocked his head at me. "Now, tell me, do you have a particular subject in mind? Because *who* it is could make a big difference."

"Helen Ralston." Until I spoke, I hadn't really known.

Plenty of well-read people would have responded, quite reasonably, with a blank stare or a puzzled shake of the head. Helen Ralston was hardly a household name, now or ever. Her fame, such as it was, rested entirely on one book. *In Troy* had been published by a small press in the 1930s and developed a kind of underground reputation, read by few but admired by those discerning readers who made the effort. In the 1960s it was published again—in America for the first time—and there was even a mass-market paperback, which is what I'd read in college. It was revived from obscurity once again by Virago in the 1980s, but, from the results of my bookstore visit before lunch, I was pretty sure it was out of print again.

Selwyn knew all this as well as I did. Not only was he a voracious reader, but before becoming an agent he'd been a book-dealer, twentieth-century first editions his specialty.

"I sold my first edition of *In Troy* to Carmen Callil," he said.

I was horrified. "Not to set from?" Reprints like the Virago Classics are photo-offset from other editions, a process that destroys the original book.

He shook his head. "No. She already had a copy of the 1964 Peter Owen edition. She wanted the first for herself. I let her have it for sixty quid. These days, I doubt you could get a first edition for under three hundred."

It always amazed me that people could remember how much they'd paid for things in the past. Such specifics eluded me. I could only remember emotionally, comparatively: something had cost *a lot* or *not much*.

"I should talk to Carmen," I said. "She probably met Helen Ralston when she decided to publish her."

"Probably." He had a thoughtful look on his face. "Didn't we talk about *In Troy* once before? When I was selling *Isis*. *In Troy* had some influence on your book, didn't it?"

I ducked my head in agreement, slightly embarrassed. *Isis* was either my first or my second novel, depending on whether you judged by date of composition or actual publication. Either way, I'd written it a life-time ago. I could hardly recall the young woman I had been when I'd started it, and by now my attitude toward that novel—once so important to me—was clear-eyed, critical, fond but distant. "Yes, it was my model. Almost too much influence, it had—I didn't realize how deeply I'd absorbed *In Troy* until my second or third revision of *Isis*. Then I had to cut out great tranches of poetic prose because it was too much like hers, and wasn't really *me* at all."

I recalled how I'd been pierced, at the age of nineteen, by the insights and language of *In Troy*. It felt at times like I was reading my own story, only written so much better than I could ever hope to match. It was such an amazingly personal book, I felt it had been written for me alone. If Helen of Troy was Helen Ralston's mythic equivalent for the purposes of her novel, then she was mine. Somehow, the author's affair with her teacher in Scotland was exactly the same as mine, fifty years later in upstate New York. Details of time, space, location and even personal identity were insignificant set in the balance with the eternal truths, the great rhythms of birth and death and change.

I had a genuine, Proustian rush then, the undeniable certainty that time could be conquered. All at once, sitting at a table in an Edinburgh restaurant, the taste of wine sharp

and fresh on my tongue, I felt myself still curled in the bas-
ket chair in that long-ago dorm room in upstate New York,
the smell of a joss-stick from my room-mate's side of the
room competing with the clove, orange, and cinnamon scent
of the cup of Constant Comment tea I sipped while I read,
the sound of Joni Mitchell on the stereo as Helen Ralston's
words blazed up at me, changing me and my world forever
with the universe-destroying, universe-creating revelation
that time is an illusion.

"I was *meant* to write this book," I said to my agent, with
all the passion and conviction of the teenager I had been
thirty-two years ago.

He didn't grin, but I caught the spark of amusement in
his eyes, and it made me scowl with self-doubt. "You think
I'm crazy?"

"No. No." He leaned across the table and put his hand
firmly on mine. "I think you sound like your old self again."

Our food arrived and we talked about other things.

The crab cakes were, indeed, superb. They were served
with a crunchy potato gallette and a delicious mixture of
seared red peppers and Spanish onion. My salad included
rocket, watercress, baby spinach, and some other tasty and
exotic leaves I couldn't identify, all tossed in a subtle, herby
balsamic dressing. When I exclaimed at it, Selwyn grinned
and shook his head.

"You should get out more. That's a standard restaurant
salad."

My nearest restaurant was a twenty-mile drive away, and
didn't suit my budget.

"I don't get out much, but I'd make this for myself, if I
could get rocket in the Co-op."

"The Co-op?" His delivery brought to mind Dame Edith

Evans uttering the immortal question—"A hand bag?"—in *The Importance of Being Earnest.*

"Does the Co-Op still exist? And you *shop* there?"

"When I must."

"Oh, my dear. When *are* you moving back to civilization?"

"I don't consider that civilization resides in consumer convenience, actually."

"No." He sounded unconvinced. "But what do you *do* out in the country? I mean, what's the great appeal?" Selwyn was such a complete urbanite, he couldn't imagine any use for countryside except to provide a quiet chill-out zone at the weekend.

"I do the same things I'd do anywhere else."

"You'd shop at the Co-Op?"

I laughed. "Well, no. But I can write anywhere."

"Of course you can. And when you're not writing, in the city, there's art galleries, theatres, bookstores . . . what is it you like about the country?"

"The hills, the sea, peace and quiet, going for walks, going sailing . . ."

He was nodding. "I remember, I remember. I grilled you on this before, when you told me you were going to marry your former editor and leave London. I couldn't understand it. *Not* the part about marrying Allan—who was a better man than the publishing world deserved—but why leave London?"

I sighed a little. "We'd decided to down-shift. Allan hated his job; I was fed up in general . . . we figured out we could sell our flats and buy a boat, spend more time together and have a better quality of life on less money there."

"It still suits you?"

I pushed a strip of red pepper around on my plate. That life had been planned for, and suited, two people. After

Allan's death I'd taken the advice of my closest friends not to rush into anything or do anything too drastic, so I hadn't moved, or made any major changes to my life. What was the point, anyway? Nothing I could do would change the only thing that really mattered.

"I couldn't afford to move back to London."

"There are other places. Don't tell the folks down south I said so, but I actually prefer Edinburgh. Or Glasgow."

"I guess you haven't checked out property prices since devolution."

"But surely if you sold your farm—"

"It's not a farm, Selwyn, it's a farm *cottage.* A dinky toy. Somebody else owns the farm and the nice big farmhouse and all the land and lets us share the farm track."

"Still, it must be worth something. Think about it. Once you start writing this book you won't want to have the hassle of moving, but you will want to be near a good library."

I thought of myself in a library, surrounded by stacks of books. The idea of having a project, things to look up, real work to do again, was incredibly seductive. "The first thing is to put together a proposal, something I can show around. Just a few basic facts, the reason Helen Ralston is of interest, the stance you're going to take, why she's well overdue for a biography—" he broke off. "There hasn't already been one, has there?"

"Not that I know of."

"Mmm. Better check the more obscure university press catalogue ... you can do that online. And ask around, just in case somebody is already working on her. It would be good to know."

My heart gave a jolt. "If there was ... couldn't I still write mine?"

"The trouble is, publishers are always ready to commission a new life of Dickens or Churchill, but nobody wants to publish two 'first' biographies in the same year—probably not even in the same decade."

Until a couple of hours ago, I hadn't given Helen Ralston more than a passing thought in years. I'd had no notion of writing her biography before lunch, and yet now it was the one thing I most wanted to do. I couldn't bear the idea of giving it up.

"How will I find out if somebody else is already doing one?"

"Don't look so tragic! If someone *has* got a commission, it may be some boring old academic who's going to take ten years, and you could get yours out first. Anyway, don't worry about it. Just have a scout around. If there's going to be a biography coming out next year, well, much better to find out now, before you've invested a lot of time and energy in it."

Forewarned wasn't necessarily forearmed, I thought. I didn't put much stock in the theory of minimizing pain that way. If I'd known in advance that Allan would die of a heart attack at the age of sixty it wouldn't have hurt any less when it happened, and it wouldn't have stopped me loving him. I did know, when I married him, that his father had died of a heart attack at sixty, and even without that genetic factor, the statistical chances were that I'd outlive him by a couple of decades. I came of sturdy peasant stock, and the women in my family were long-lived.

"How do I scout around? I mean, who do I talk to?"

"You could start with her."

"Her? You mean Helen Ralston?"

He was surprised by my surprise. "She is still alive?"

"Is she? She'd be awfully old."

"Ninety-six or ninety-seven. Not impossible. I don't remember seeing an obituary of her in the last few years."

"Me either. I'm sure I would have noticed. Well. I guess they might still have an address for her at Virago. And there's a biography of Willy Logan, quite new, that should have something." I patted the heavy square shape of it in the bag slung across the side of my chair.

"Dessert? No? Coffee?" He summoned the waiter and, when he'd gone away again, turned back to me. "By the way, I know someone who owns one of Helen Ralston's paintings."

"'By the way'?"

He smiled. "Really, I just remembered. And he lives here in Edinburgh. An old friend. I should probably call in on him while I'm here—are you free for the rest of this afternoon, or do you have to rush off?"

"I'm free. Do you mean it? I'd love to see it!"

I felt a little stunned by this sudden unexpected bonus. While Selwyn got out his phone and made the call I tried to imagine what a Helen Ralston painting would look like. Although I knew she'd been an art student, I thought of her always as a writer, and I'd never seen so much as a description of one of her paintings. That it should have fallen into my lap like this, before I'd even started work, did not strike me as odd or unusual. Everyone who writes or researches knows that this sort of serendipity—the chance discovery, the perfectly timed meeting, the amazing coincidence—is far from rare. The fact that this first one had come along so soon, before I was definitely committed to the project, just confirmed my feeling: I was *meant* to write this book.

Selwyn's friend lived a short cab ride away in an area known as The Colonies. This was a collection of quaint, tidy little cottages set in eleven parallel terraces, built, he told me, in 1861 to provide affordable housing for respectable artisans and their families, and now much in demand among singles and young professional couples for their central location and old-fashioned charm.

The sight of these neat little houses set out like a model village in narrow, cobbled streets roused the long-dormant American tourist in me, and before I could crush her down again I was gushing, "Ooh, they're so *cute*!"

The big black cab had to stop on the corner to let us out, as it clearly would not be able to turn around if it went any further.

"They're just adorable!" I became more excited as I noticed the window boxes and trim green lawns. In its day, this had been inexpensive housing, but that hadn't translated into an ugly utilitarianism. The houses were small—I couldn't imagine how they'd ever been thought suitable for the large families people had in the old days—but their proportions were appealing to the eye, and they didn't look cramped. "What a great place to live—so quiet and pretty, like a village, but right in the middle of the city. You could walk everywhere from here, or bike, you wouldn't even need a car."

Selwyn was looking amused. "I'll get Alistair to let you know as soon as one comes on the market. They're very much in demand, but with advance notice maybe you could put in a preemptive bid."

"I didn't mean *I* wanted to live here—" but as I spoke, I thought again. Why shouldn't it be me living the life I'd suddenly glimpsed, in a small, neat, pretty house or a flat within an ancient city? I still loved the country, but after all, there were trains and buses for whenever I wanted a day out, and these days I was feeling distinctly more starved of culture than I was of fresh air and wide open spaces.

"Well," I said, changing tack, "if you can re-launch my career, I will definitely think about re-launching my life."

He draped an arm loosely about my shoulders and led me gently down the street. "*We*—the operative word is *we*—are going to re-launch your career, big-time. Turn in at the green gate."

The house where Selwyn's friend lived was divided into two residences, top and bottom. His was upstairs, the front door reached by a rather elegant sweeping curve of stairs.

A thin, neat, very clean-looking old man opened the door to us. This was Alistair Reid. He had a long nose and slightly protuberant bright blue eyes in a reddish, taut-skinned face. His cheeks were as shiny as apples—I imagined him buffing them every morning—and his sleeked back hair was cream-colored.

"I've just put the kettle on," he said, leading us into his sitting room. "Indian, or China?"

He was looking at me. I looked at Selwyn.

"China, if you've got it."

"I should hardly make the offer if I hadn't got it," the old man said reprovingly. But despite his tone there was a twinkle in his eye, so I guessed it was meant to be a joke. "Please, make yourselves at home. I'll not be long," he said as he left us.

I looked around the room, which was light and airy and beautifully furnished. It was clear even to my untutored eye that the delicate writing table beside the window, the glass-fronted bookcase in the corner, and the dark chest beside the door were all very old, finely made, unique pieces that were undoubtedly very expensive. Even the couch where Selwyn and I perched had a solidity and individuality about it that suggested it had not been mass-produced.

The pale walls were hung with paintings. I got up and went to look at them. One wall displayed a series of watercolor landscapes, the usual Scottish scenes of mountains, water, cloud-streaked skies and island-dotted seas. They were attractive enough, yet rather bland; more accomplished than my own attempts, but nothing special.

Beside the bookcase were two still-lifes in oils: one, very realistic and very dark, looked old; I guessed it could be two or three hundred years old. It depicted a large dead fish lying on a marble slab with a bundle of herbs and, incongruously, a single yellow flower. The other painting was much more modern in style, an arrangement of a blue bowl, dull silver spoon, and bright yellow lemon on a surface in front of a window, partly visible behind a blue and white striped curtain.

The largest painting in the room had a whole wall to itself. It was the portrait of a young woman. She had smartly bobbed hair and wore a long single strand of pearls against a dark green tunic. I stared at this picture for some time before noticing that it was signed in the lower left-hand corner with the initials W.E.L.

Alistair Reid came in with a tray, which he set down on

a small table near the couch. I went back to take a seat and saw, with some dismay, that besides the tea he'd brought a plate of thinly sliced, liberally buttered white bread and another plate piled high with small, iced cakes.

"From Tesco's, I'm afraid," he said in his soft, lilting voice. "But I can recommend them. They're really rather nice. Or would you rather have sandwiches? I wasn't sure. It won't take me a moment to make them if you'd like. Ham, or cheese, or anchovy paste, or tomato."

"Thank you, Alistair, you're more than kind, but we've just had lunch," Selwyn said. He turned to me. "You know the old joke, that in Glasgow unexpected afternoon visitors are greeted with the cry of 'You'll be wanting your tea, then,' whereas in Edinburgh, no matter the time, it's always, 'You'll have had your tea, then.'" He shot a grin in the old man's direction. "Well, I should have warned you, but Alistair has devoted his *life* to disproving that calumny on the hospitable souls of native Edinburghers."

"Oh, go on, I know you've a sweet tooth," Alistair said, not quite smiling.

"Well, I think I might just manage a fancy or two," said Selwyn.

I took a slice of bread and butter and eventually allowed a cake to be pressed upon me, glad that we'd skipped dessert. The tea was light and delicate, flavored with jasmine blossoms.

Alistair leaned towards me. "I believe when I came in I saw you admiring the portrait of my mother?"

"That was your mother? Painted by W. E. Logan?"

He nodded, eyelids drooping a little. "Long before I was born, of course. Her father commissioned it in 1926. It was quite possibly the last portrait W. E. Logan ever painted, apart from some studies of Helen Ralston, of course." He gestured towards the watercolor landscapes. "And those are my mother's."

"Your mother was an artist, too?"

He shook his head. "Oh, no. My mother painted purely for her own enjoyment. I have them on display because they remind me of her and because of where they were painted. It's where we always took our summer holidays, on the west coast, in Argyll."

"That's where I'm from!"

"Really? I'd have guessed you're from much further west." A teasing smile flickered about his thin lips.

I felt a little weary and tried not to show it. No matter how long I lived in Britain—and it was now nearly a quarter of a century—I could never pass for native. As soon as I opened my mouth I was a foreigner, always required to account for my past. Yet I didn't want to be unkind or rude, and it wasn't fair to take offence where none was intended. Scots, unlike some other Europeans, were generally fond of Americans.

"I was born in Texas," I said. "Later I lived in New York, and then London. I've been living in Argyll for just over ten years. It's a tiny little place called Mealdarroch, not far from—"

"But that's exactly where we stayed!" he exclaimed. "It was always Mealdarroch, or Ardfern." Looking delighted, he turned to Selwyn. "My dear, how marvelous! You never said you were bringing someone from Mealdarroch! My favorite spot in the universe!" He turned back to me. "You sail, of course."

"We—I—have a boat. My husband loved to sail. Since he died, I haven't felt like taking her out on my own."

"Oh, my dear, I am so sorry." His sharp blue eyes were suddenly gentle.

I looked down at my teacup, into the light gold liquid, and thought of how one might re-create that color in a watercolor wash. After a moment I could face him again, quite calm.

"I was looking at your pictures trying to guess which one was by Helen Ralston. But if the watercolors are your mother's, and the portrait by Logan—"

His eyes widened. "Oh, that's not hanging in here! I could hardly have it on display to all and sundry—far too risky!"

I thought at first he was speaking of *risk* before I realized he meant the painting itself was *risqué*—did he mean it was a nude figure? But nudes had been common currency in fine art for a long time and surely were acceptable even in buttoned-down Calvinist Scotland?

Alistair turned to Selwyn. "Didn't you explain?"

"I thought she'd better see for herself."

I tried to imagine it. Had Helen Ralston turned the tables on the male-dominated art world and depicted her lover in the altogether? Willy Logan and his little willy? And if it wasn't so little, or dangling...? The erect penis was taboo even today.

"May I see it?"

"But of course. Drink up your tea. Sure you won't have another fancy cake? No? Selwyn? Oh, go on, dear boy, no one cares about your figure now!"

We went out by the door we had come in, back into the tiny entrance-way, where a steep, narrow staircase rose to the left.

"Go halfway up the stair," Alistair instructed. "It's too narrow for more than one person at a time. You'll see it hanging on the wall just at the turn of the stair."

It certainly was narrow and steep. Maybe that was the reason for the inclusion of the little half-landing, to give the intrepid climber a space to pause and make a 90° turn before mounting to the floor above.

The picture hung on the wall that faced the second flight of stairs. It was about 8" x 10", or the size of a standard sheet of paper torn from an artist's pad. I saw a watercolor land-scape, not so very different from the pictures hanging in the room downstairs.

Then there was a click from the hall below, and the shaded bulb above my head blazed, illuminating the picture.

I gazed at the painted image of an island, a rocky island rendered loosely in shades of brown and green and grey and greyish pink. I remained unimpressed, and baffled by Alistair's attitude towards this uninspired daub. *Risky?*

And then, all at once, as if another light had been switched on, I saw the hidden picture. Within the contours of the island was a woman. A woman, naked, on her back, her knees up and legs splayed open, her face hidden by a forearm flung across it and by the long hair—greenish, greyish—that flowed around her like the sea.

The centre of the painting, what drew the eye and com-manded the attention, was the woman's vulva: all the life of the painting was concentrated there. A slash of pink, startling against the mossy greens and browns, seemed to touch a nerve in my own groin.

One immediate, furious thought rose in my mind: *How could she expose herself like that?*

Somehow I knew this was a self-portrait, that the artist would not have exploited another woman in this way. Yet she had not flinched from depicting *herself* as naked, passive, open, sexually receptive—no, sexually voracious, demanding to be looked at, to be taken, explored, used, filled . . .

Well, why not? I was all in favor of female autonomy, in

the freedom of women to act out of their own desires, whatever they were. After all, I still called myself a feminist, and I had come of age during the '60s, a member of the post-Pill, pre-AIDS, sexually liberated generation who believed in letting it all hang out, and a woman's right to choose.

And yet—and yet—

Whatever theory I held, the sight of this picture made me cringe away in revulsion, even fear. As if this was something I should not have seen, something that should not have been revealed. It was deeper than reason; I simply felt there was something wrong and *dangerous* in this painting.

Then, like a cloud passing across the sun, the atmosphere changed again. Outlines blurred, colors became drab, and abruptly the painting was only the depiction of an island in the sea.

But I knew now what was hidden in those rocky outlines, and I didn't trust it to stay hidden. I turned away immediately and saw the two men standing at the bottom of the stairs, looking up at me.

There was a sudden rush of blood to my head: my cheeks burned. They knew what I'd been looking at; they'd seen it, too. And then, far worse than the embarrassment, came a clutch of fear, because I was a woman, and my only way out was blocked by two men.

The moment passed. The old man went back into the other room, and I was looking down at Selwyn, whom I'd known for twenty years.

I hated the fact that I was blushing, but I'd look even more of a fool if I hovered there on the landing waiting for the red to fade, so I went down. Unostentatiously polite as ever, he turned away, allowing me to follow him into the sitting room where Alistair waited for us.

Selwyn cleared his throat. "Well—"

"Sit down," said the old man. "You'll want to hear the story. First, let me fetch down the picture. There's something written on the back that you should see."

In uneasy silence, we sat down. The silence was uneasy on my part, anyway, as I struggled to understand my own reaction. I was not a prude, and although hardcore porn made me uncomfortable, mere nudity didn't. I had no problem, usually, with images of healthy female bodies, and I'd seen beaver shots before, far more graphic than Helen Ralston's *trompe-l'oeil* depiction.

In the nineteenth century Gustave Courbet had painted a detailed, close-up, highly realistic view of a woman's pubic area, calling it "The Origin of the World." At the time, this was a deeply shocking thing to have done, and although Courbet was a well-respected artist, the painting could not be shown. Now, of course, it could be seen by anyone who cared to call up a reproduction on the internet, purchased in museum shops all over the world as a postcard or poster, and for all I knew it was available on T-shirts and mouse mats, too.

Courbet's realistic depiction was far more graphic than Ralston's impressionistic watercolor, and it might be argued that, as a male artist, he was objectifying women, serving her sexual parts up on canvas for the viewing pleasure of his fellow men, whereas Ralston had been exploring her own feelings about herself with, possibly, no intention of ever having it on public display. The question I should have been asking myself was why, when Courbet's picture did not disturb me, hers *did*.

Alistair returned, carrying the picture. He handed it to me, face down, and I took it, gingerly, awkwardly, into my lap.

"I had it mounted with a bit cut away at the back so you can still see what she wrote," he explained.

I looked down and had my first sight of Helen Ralston's bold, clear handwriting:

My Death
April 14, 1929
This, like all I own or produce, is for
My Beloved Willy
HER

I shivered and made to pass it to Selwyn, but he demurred: he'd seen it before. So I went on holding it in my lap, feeling it slowly burning a hole in me, and looked at Alistair.

"Why 'My Death'? Did she mean ... sexuality equates with death?"

He spread his hands. "Much more than that, I'm sure. The two of them used certain words almost as if they were a special code, and capital-D Death was one of them. And consider the painting: the woman is also an island. A particular island, from your part of the world," he added with a nod at me. "In fact, I must have sailed past it many times myself on our family holidays, although I don't think we ever landed there. According to Willy Logan in his memoirs, the moment she set eyes upon the island she declared, 'I've seen my death.' Whether 'my death' meant the same as capital-D Death to them, I couldn't say, but clearly it wasn't perceived as a threat or I'm sure they would have sailed away, rather than dropping anchor and going ashore, full of excitement, to explore."

I knew that in the Tarot the Death card did not signify physical demise, but rather meant a sudden, dramatic change of fortune. And sometimes people had to dare death in order to regain their lives. I wondered if Helen Ralston had been a precursor of Sylvia Plath, if she was another Lady Lazarus, making death her life's art. First, out a window into the air; the second time, on a rocky island...

"What happened? Did something happen there?"

"Logan went blind," Selwyn told me.

I had known, of course, that Logan had lost his sight—the transformation of a rather dull society painter into the blind poetic visionary was the most famous thing about him. But I didn't know how it had happened. "On the island? Some sort of accident?"

"No accident," said Alistair crisply. "Haven't you read *Touched by the Goddess*? You must read Logan's memoirs. His explanation...well, it's hardly satisfactory, but it's all we have. No one will ever know what *really* happened."

Had Logan intervened somehow? I wondered. Had the Death waiting for Helen been made to give her up, but taken Logan's sight in exchange? It was clear that Alistair wasn't going to tell—if he knew.

"How did you come to have the painting?" Selwyn asked.

"You know I was an art and antiques dealer back in the 1970s and '80s. Torquil Logan—Willy's youngest son—was on the fringe of the trade himself, and that was how we knew each other. When the old man died, although his literary agent was the executor of his estate, it was the sons and daughters who did all the donkey work of clearing out his things and deciding what should be sold, or given away, shipped to the library that was to have the official collection, or whatever. Torquil got in touch with me when he came across *My Death*—it was in an envelope at the back of a file of old letters and probably had not been seen in fifty years.

"He knew what it was, straight away. Well, of course: it was described in *Touched by the Goddess* right down to the inscription on the back, and invested with huge significance as the last work of art he ever looked at, the final gift from his mistress/muse, and even as a sort of premonition of what was about to happen to him, his blinding by the Goddess.

"And Torquil didn't know what to do with it. *He* didn't want it; in fact, he told me, he felt a sort of revulsion about the very thought of having it in his house. He couldn't ask his mother—she was in poor health and quite devastated by the loss of her husband; he didn't want to take any risks by even reminding her in any way of the existence of Helen Ralston. He'd considered leaving it in the envelope and slipping it into one of the boxes destined for the library—it would be safe enough in a university collection, he thought, and yet the idea of students looking at it and writing about it in their theses made him feel queasy, just as did the thought of it going into a public auction, to be numbered and listed and described in a catalogue."

Alistair paused and took a deep breath. Then he went on. "I offered to take care of it for him. I promised there'd be no publicity. In fact, I said, if the price was right, I'd be happy to buy it for myself, not to sell on. Torq knew, because we'd talked about it, just how important Willy Logan's books had been to me. Especially as a young man. That mystical strand of his, the idea that the old gods are still alive in the land and can be brought back to life through us, *in* us—I can't quite explain how deeply that affected me, but the idea of owning something that had belonged to him, which had been so deeply, personally meaningful, was irresistible.

"And Torquil said I could have it. In fact, he said he would like to *give* it to me. He didn't want payment; it didn't seem right to sell it. I protested, but he wouldn't hear of it. In fact, he mailed it to me that same day, by ordinary post, in a padded envelope, but otherwise unprotected—when I think how easily it could have been lost or damaged..."

We all stared at the thing in my lap. Unable to bear it any longer, I lifted the framed painting like a tray and held it out to Alistair. When he didn't respond, I glared at him, but still he made no move to take it away.

"I could never sell it," he said quietly. "I've respected Torquil's feelings about that. And yet, I've never felt right about owning it. It came to me by chance." He paused. His tongue appeared at the corner of his mouth and ran quickly around his lips. "I'd like you to have it."

"Me!" I felt the same unexpectedly sexual shock I'd had on first recognizing the hidden meaning of the picture I now held. "Oh, no, I couldn't. It's not right."

"Selwyn tells me you're writing a biography of Helen Ralston. I've felt for some time that the painting should go back to her, but I didn't know how to approach her. It seemed too difficult, and potentially too disturbing. How would she feel to learn that a male stranger had this very personal thing? Yet she might want it back. And it *is* hers, by rights, since Willy's death. It might come more easily from another woman, and, as her biographer, you'll be in on lots of intimate secrets; she'll have to accept that..."

"I don't know that she'll even accept me as her biographer. I can't. I don't even know if she's still alive." I couldn't seem to stop shaking my head.

"Of course she will. Of course she is. And if she doesn't want it, or you can't find her, and you don't feel you can keep it yourself, well, you could always mail it back to me in a plain brown envelope. Please."

And although I really didn't want to do it, in the end I found it impossible not to agree.

I'd booked a room for the night at Jurys hotel, which was located just behind the train station. I'd planned, when I'd booked, to take myself out for a nice dinner and to see a movie, but by the time I'd parted from Selwyn, very late in the afternoon, the only thing I wanted was to find out more about Helen Ralston.

I hit another bookshop, where I determined that *In Troy* was definitely out of print, and so was that old-fashioned children's classic *Hermine in Cloud-Land*. "But you can find loads of second-hand copies on the internet," a helpful clerk assured me.

"Thanks, I'll do that when I get home," I said, and paid for a copy of *Touched by the Goddess*. I bought a selection of interesting-looking gourmet salads from Marks and Spencer —ah, the luxuries of city life!—and settled into my hotel room to read everything in the big fat biography of Willy Logan that had anything to do with Helen Ralston.

SHE WAS the girl from far away, the girl from another land, and she swept into the dreich damp grey streets of Glasgow like a warm wind, smelling of exotic spices and a hint of dangerous mystery. She claimed to be half-Greek and half-Irish, with a mother who told fortunes and a father possessed of the second sight. She herself, according to at least one bewildered classmate, was subject to "fits" when she would go rigid and begin to prophesy in a voice manifestly not her own—afterwards, she appeared exhausted and claimed to remember nothing.

In appearance, she made a most unlikely *femme fatale*. She was small and skinny, with sharp features, including a prominent nose, and her eyes, although large and lustrous, were disturbingly deep-set. Logan's portrait glamorized her; the few photographs taken of Helen Ralston in the late 1920s reveal an odd shrunken figure who appeared prematurely old.

Helen Elizabeth Ralston was a new student on the rolls of the Glasgow School of Art in September 1927; prior to that she had studied at Syracuse University, New York. Her reasons for departing New York for Glasgow are unknown. She had no Scottish connections whatsoever, and was far from wealthy. Although her tuition fees were paid in advance, she clearly found it a struggle to pay for supplies and other necessities of life. A fellow student, Mabel Scott Smith, who recalls buying her dinner more than once, made it a practice to bring along an extra bun for Helen at tea time: "She would pretend she'd forgotten, or that she wasn't hungry, but the truth was, she didn't have a penny to spare. Everybody knew she was broke, even though you thought Americans must all be rich. She went around with a portfolio of drawings, trying to sell to the papers, but she never had a hope. She was good, but so were plenty others, and times were hard. It was even worse in Glasgow than in other places; you couldn't make money from pretty pictures there, not then."

The budding friendship between Mabel and Helen came to an abrupt end when the American student moved out of her shared lodgings and into a West End flat paid for by W. E. Logan. Mabel Smith: "It wasn't the sex—we art school girls had quite a liberal attitude towards that!—but that she would let herself be *kept* and by a married man! I lost my respect for Mr Logan, too."

Logan noticed the "young-old" quality of Helen Ralston's face during his first class with her, and invited her to sit for him on Saturday afternoon. He singled out several students like this every year; there was nothing unusual, or improper, in his attentions. But from her first sitting it was clear that Helen would be different. Fixing her large, hypnotic eyes upon him, she began to speak and immediately held him spell-bound by her stories.

These were probably mostly a retelling of myths and legends from many different cultures, Russian fairy-tales mingled with Greek myths, and Celtic motifs interwoven with material stolen from the Arabian Nights. To Logan they were pure magic, igniting in him the passion for myth that would dominate his life.

In his autobiography Logan writes of certain "magical" moments in his early childhood. Apart from that, however, there is no evidence that he experienced any significant mystical or spiritual leanings before meeting Helen Ralston.

Despite the stories she told him about her background, Helen Elizabeth Ralston had neither Greek nor Irish blood. Her parents, Ben and Sadie Rudinski, were Polish Jews who arrived in New York around 1890. By the time their last child, Helen, was born in Brooklyn in 1907, the family fortunes were thriving. Helen's artistic ambitions were encouraged, and she was both educated and indulged. As America prepared to go to war in 1917, the Rudinskis changed their name to Ralston—around this time, Helen adopted Elizabeth as a middle name and began signing her drawings with the initials HER.

Helen did well at school and was accepted into the undergraduate liberal arts program at Syracuse University. Her grades from her freshman year were good, and she participated in the drama society (painting sets and making costumes rather than acting) and contributed to the student newspaper and seemed in general to have settled. But instead of returning as expected for a second year, Helen Elizabeth Ralston applied to the Glasgow School of Art, and embarked on a new life in Great Britain.

Logan wrote later that she made this great change in her life on the prompting of a dream. He also believed that her parents were dead, that she was an only child, and that she had been self-supporting since the age of thirteen. It is impossible to know for certain when the relationship between them altered and they became lovers, as Logan is uncharacteristically reticent about this in his memoirs. But by January 1928 he had begun to paint *Circe*, and by March she was living in the flat for which he paid the rent, and to which he was a frequent visitor.

After January, although she did not formally withdraw from the School, Helen attended fewer and fewer classes, until, by March, the other students scarcely saw her at all, unless she was in Logan's company. Their relationship was certainly gossiped about, but Logan's reputation was such that some thought him above suspicion. He was a respectable family man, with several children and a beautiful, gentle wife from a well-to-do Edinburgh background. The American student was such an odd creature it was hard to credit that the great W. E. Logan was seriously attracted to her.

He had often taken a paternal interest in his students, male and female, and had even been known to make small financial contributions to help support those who were talented but poor. Helen Ralston clearly fell into that category. Brian Ross, Logan's biographer, suggested that Logan's natural innocence combined with generosity and good intentions might have got him into trouble. He thought that Helen had fallen in love with the great man, who had been interested in her only as a model. When *Circe* was finished, and it became clear that he would no longer be spending so much time alone in the studio with her, she had thrown herself out of the window in despair, and only then had he become aware of her true feelings for him.

I shut Ross's book in disgust. In the whole history of human relationships, how many men had ever rented an expensive flat for an unrelated female without expecting sexual favors in return? If she'd been one-sidedly in love with him, her suicide attempt would have been his signal to run like hell, not to abandon wife and children to nurse her back to health. Logan's sacrifice only made sense if he was deeply in love with her, and her leap had shocked him into recognizing his responsibilities.

I was willing to believe that it had been one-sided—on *his* part. She might have stopped going to art school to avoid him, even though her poverty had forced her into accepting his financial support, and she might have hoped that, once he no longer needed her to model for *Circe* she would have nothing more to do with him. Only he wouldn't let her go—maybe he'd turned up that August day not to say good-bye, but to tell her he was going to leave his wife and children to live with her. I imagined her backing away from him, evading his hands, his lips, his unwanted declarations of undying devotion until, in a last, desperate squirm out of his arms, she'd fallen out of the window.

I frowned as I considered this. What sort of window was it? How did a conscious, healthy adult fall out of a window? I found it hard to visualize from Ross's description—he said she was "sitting on the window ledge." Sideways, or with her back to the air? It was August, and hot, so naturally enough the windows were open. Did she lean too far back and lose her balance, or did she deliberately swivel around and jump?

I picked up *Touched by the Goddess* and paged through it looking for references to Hermine, which was his name for Helen. There was no index. One reference leaped out at me:

> Truth then flying out the window, Hermine went after it. She caught it, although she nearly died in the attempt, and so restored me to the way of truth, and life.

Well, that was a lot of help. Logan was concerned with myth, as he saw it, a deeper truth than mere facts could provide.

I turned back to Ross again. It seemed that, however

briefly, an attempted murder charge had been considered, on the grounds of Logan's distraught "confession" to a policeman at the hospital to which Helen had been taken. Undoubtedly, he'd been filled with feelings of guilt, but was it the guilt of a violent seducer, or that of a man who felt torn between two women, or simply what anyone close to an attempted suicide might feel? Even his actual words at the time were unclear. And, as Ross pointed out, suicide was a crime, so Logan might have been trying to save Helen from prosecution and/or deportation for attempted self-murder by suggesting it was really his fault.

More than one story could be told about what had happened in that room in Glasgow, a room with an open window, four storeys up, on a warm August day in 1928. There had been only two witnesses, who were also the protagonists, or the protagonist and the antagonist, the two people in the room, Willy Logan and Helen Ralston.

Ross wrote far more clearly and simply than Logan in his attempt to establish the truth, but, as far as I could see, he was no less biased, and no more reliable, because there was only one story he wanted to tell, and that was Willy Logan's. Helen's experience, her interpretation, her story, was nowhere in his book.

I went back to the beginning and made my way carefully through the acknowledgements. This ran to over two pages of names of all the people who had helped him in some way, and Helen Ralston's name was not included. If she was dead, I thought, he might have quoted from one of her books or letters—surely she had written about her relationship with Logan at some point, to someone? Some of the passages from *In Troy* could well have been pertinent. His restraint made me think he must have been refused permission to quote, with possibly the threat of legal action if he said anything about her that could be deemed offensive ... the libel laws in Britain were pretty fierce, and if the old lady had a taste for litigation that would have tied his hands.

I read swiftly through the pages that dealt with Logan's desertion of his family, his devoted vigils beside Helen's hospital bed, the loss of his job scarcely registering on him, her surgery, the creation of little Hermine and her adventures, then Helen's convalescence in the West End flat, now *their* home, until, in the spring of 1929, although she still had to walk with a cane, Helen was deemed well enough to travel, and Logan took her on a sailing holiday up the west coast. In the fresh air away from the city they would rest and sketch and grow strong, Willy wrote in a letter to his son Torquil, adding:

> I hope you know how much I love you, darling boy, and that I don't stay away out of crossness or dislike or any wrong reason, but only because Helen needs me so much more than the rest of you do. She has been very ill, you know, but finally is getting better. I hope soon she will be well enough to meet you. I have written and drawn a funny little story for her which I think you will like, too. It is to be published as a book in September, and I have told the publishers to be sure to send you your very own copy...

On their first day out, they spotted a small island. In Logan's description, Helen went "rigid," her face paled, and her large, shiny eyes seemed to become even larger, a trio of symptoms that had always heralded her prophesying fits. This time all she said was, "I've seen my death. My death is there."

Logan never explained why, in that case, he didn't just sail as far away from the island as he could. To him, it was self-evidently necessary to go where Helen had foreseen her own death. In his novel *In Circe's Snare* (1948) Logan has Odysseus declare, "Every man must seek his own death."

"And every woman, too," Circe chimed in quickly. "If, that is, she wishes to be more than just a woman."

On the charts the island bears the name of Eilean nan Achlan. At the time, this probably meant nothing to Logan, but later, when he began his study of Gaelic, he would have found that it bears the meaning "the isle of lamentation."

Modern archeologists believe that Achlan was an important funerary site in pre-Christian Scotland. Not only the name points to this conclusion, but the many cairns, including one large chambered tomb, still awaiting serious excavation today, believed to have been in use for a period of several hundred years. There was a tradition for a long time on the west coast of interring the dead on uninhabited islands reserved for that purpose. More often these islands were located in lakes or inland lochs, but Achlan's position in the straits of Jura, relatively near to the mainland shore, would have made it equally accessible and therefore suitable for this purpose.

Because it was late in the day, they did not attempt to land just then, but dropped anchor and spent the night on board in view of the little island. While the light was good they both made watercolor sketches of it. What Logan thought of his own painting—the last he would ever produce—or what became of it is not recorded. But, as Logan recalled in *Touched by the Goddess*, Helen's swiftly rendered landscape was "technically remarkably assured, and quite surprising; the most remarkable piece of work I ever saw her produce." He expressed his belief that already "the Goddess was working through her." On the back of the little sketch she wrote the title "My Death," the date—14 April 1929—and a dedication to her lover.

Reading this, I was quite certain that Brian Ross had never set eyes on the painting he seemed to describe. The passage was footnoted; I looked it up and read, "The current whereabouts of this painting is unknown. Personal correspondence with Torquil Logan."

I looked across the room where the painting now lay in a plain brown envelope. Alistair would have been happy to give me the frame, but I thought it would be too much to cart around. After all, I didn't intend to hang it, but just return it to the woman who had painted it.

The morning of 15 April 1929 dawned calm and fine. The sun was shining, the air warm for April, and quite still: perfect weather for exploring the island. Helen stripped off her clothes, wrapped them in a Sou'wester to make a waterproof bundle she could carry on top of her head, and slipped over the side of the boat while Willy was still blinking sleep from his eyes. She gave a sudden sharp hiss as the salt water hit her scarred back and legs: the sight of those raw, red wounds against her pale flesh seemed to reproach Willy, and although the water was not very deep he felt obliged to follow her lead and strip completely rather than just removing shoes and trousers as he would have preferred.

Naked as Adam and Eve they emerged from the sea to set foot on their new Eden. As they travelled inland, the two noticed signs of ancient human activity everywhere: burial mounds, standing stones, and slabs covered with the obsessively repeated cup and ring markings that appear throughout the west of Scotland and Ireland, their ancient significance long forgotten. Eventually they came upon the ruins of some old building, and a well. Although it was more likely to have been either an enclosure for sheep, or an early Christian hermit's cell, Logan decided their find was a "shrine" or "temple," and proclaimed this the *omphalos* of the island where they would rest, and drink the good fresh water, and give thanks to the Goddess.

In later years, Willy Logan would connect the Gaelic *Achlan* with the ancient Greek *Aeaea*, "wailing," the name of the "typical death island" that was the home of the enchantress Circe.

After their pagan prayers, they made love within the boundaries of the shrine. According to his much later account, this act was at Helen's urging and was the first sexual intercourse they'd had since her fall. Yet all did not go as planned. Reading between the lines, it appears that Willy was unable to sustain an erection. Determined to please his mistress, he had to use "other means." Oral sex is fairly obviously implied. He brought his lover to orgasm—his surprise suggests that this, too, may have been a first—and almost immediately after that, darkness fell. His lover's transformed, contorted face was the last thing he ever saw.

An annihilating blow, for an artist to lose his sight, and this event became the centre of the myth that Willy Logan was to create of his life. Although it was a moment of terror, in his writing he would describe it in terms more of awe than of fear, and of discovery and re-birth rather than of death and loss.

"The Goddess is come!" he cried (or so he claims, in his autobiography). "Oh, how she dazzles!" Then: "Where is She? Where is the sun? Is it night?" So suddenly, orgasmically,

W. E. Logan had been plunged into perpetual night, yet spiritually, he might have said, "I was blind, but now can see."

With *Touched by the Goddess* open beside *Second Chance at Life*, it was easy to see how closely Ross followed Logan's own account. Yet although he did not accept every detail uncritically, he did no more than provide a slightly ironic commentary as counterpoint to Logan's "facts." No matter how I struggled and searched, I could find no other voice, no other view, but Logan's. Helen's absence was glaring. In Logan's own autobiography, Helen was less an individual than an idea, and in Ross's book she was scarcely even that.

Yet she had certainly been there on the island; and if Logan wanted to blame her for his blindness (I was shocked by his choosing to quote, without irony, a sixteenth century Arabian scholar who declared that any man who looked into a woman's vagina would go blind), he had also to recognize that she had saved him.

While Willy wept and raved about the Goddess, Helen managed to get him back onto the boat, which she then sailed, single-handed, into Crinan Harbour. (And where, I wondered, had the girl from New York learned to sail?)

Fortunately for them, a doctor from Glasgow was staying with his wife in the Crinan Hotel—and the wife turned out to be some sort of second-cousin to Logan's mother. They immediately offered to cut short their holiday and drive Logan and Helen to Glasgow, where he could be seen by specialists.

By the time they reached Glasgow, Logan was almost supernaturally calm. He had accepted his blindness, he was convinced it was permanent and that nothing could be done about it. But his wish to go home with Helen was overruled. A bed was found for him at the Western Infirmary and arrangements were made for a battery of tests and examinations by a variety of specialists as soon as possible.

In the meantime, all were agreed, he must rest. Once she'd seen him settled in, Helen Ralston went to the nearest post office to dispatch a telegram to Mrs William Logan, whom she knew to be staying with the children and her parents in Edinburgh.

> WILLY BLIND PLEASE COME AT ONCE
> GLASGOW WESTERN INFIRMARY

She did not sign the telegram. As soon as it was sent, she went to the flat she'd shared with Willy and packed her bags. She left Glasgow that night, on a train bound for London, and never saw or directly communicated with Willy Logan again.

What would make someone who had painted a sexually explicit portrait of herself, dedicating it to her beloved, abandon that same man, blind and helpless, only twenty-four hours later? Brian Ross did not speculate or comment. I wondered who she went to in London.

I checked the index for further references to Helen Ralston. There were only a few, and every one of them concerned something Logan had written later about their brief time together (most of them clustered in the chapter about the writing of *Touched by the Goddess* in 1956). You'd never know from this book that Helen Ralston had ever done or been anything of the slightest importance in the world except to be, for a little while, Logan's chief muse and model. None of her books were listed in the "Selected Bibliography" at the end, not even *In Troy*.

I became all the more determined to tell Helen Ralston's story.

I DIDN'T sleep well that night—I rarely do, away from home. I had brief, disturbing dreams. The one that frightened me most, making me wake with a gasp and a pounding heart, was about *My Death*. I dreamed that when I got home and took the picture out to look at it, I found it was just an ordinary watercolor sketch of island, sea, and sky, no more unusual or accomplished than one of my own.

I don't know why that should have been so terrifying— especially considering how upsetting I'd found the hidden picture—but when I woke, heart pounding like a drum, it was impossible to put it out of my mind. I had to get up and look at the picture again to be sure I hadn't imagined the whole thing.

At first sight it was an island, but as I waited, staring through sleep-blurred eyes, the outlines underwent the same, subtle shift I'd seen before, and I was looking down at a woman lying with her legs splayed open. This time the sight was not so disturbing, maybe because I'd been expecting it, maybe because this time I was alone, half-asleep, naked myself, and feeling a certain amount of indignant sisterly support for a fellow writer who'd practically been written out of history.

I put the picture away, oddly comforted, and went back to bed, reflecting on the oddness of dreams.

In the jumbled, fragmented memories I carry from my childhood there are probably nearly as many dreams as images from waking life. I thought of one that might have been my earliest remembered nightmare. I was probably about four years old—I don't think I'd started school yet—when I woke up screaming. The image I retained of the dream, the thing that had frightened me so, was an ugly, clown-like doll made of soft red- and cream-colored rubber. When you squeezed it, bulbous eyes popped out on stalks and the mouth opened in a gaping scream. As I recall it now, it was disturbingly ugly, not really an appropriate toy for a very young child, but it had been mine when I was younger, at least until I'd bitten its nose off, at which point it had been taken away from me. At the time when I had the dream I hadn't seen it for a year or more—I don't think I consciously remembered it until its sudden looming appearance in a dream had frightened me awake.

When I told my mother about the dream, she was puzzled.

"But what's scary about that? You were never scared of that doll."

I shook my head, meaning that the doll I'd owned—and barely remembered—had never scared me. "But it was very scary," I said, meaning that the reappearance of it in my dream had been terrifying.

My mother looked at me, baffled. "But it's *not* scary," she said gently. I'm sure she was trying to make me feel better and thought this reasonable statement would help. She was absolutely amazed when it had the opposite result, and I burst into tears.

Of course she had no idea why, and of course I couldn't explain. Now I think—and of course I could be wrong—that what upset me was that I'd just realized that my mother and

I were separate people. We didn't share the same dreams or nightmares. I was alone in the universe, like everybody else. In some confused way, *that* was what the doll had been telling me. Once it had loved me enough to let me eat its nose; now it would make me wake up screaming.

AS SOON as I was home and through the back door, sorrow was on me like an untrained, wet and smelly dog.

My kitchen smelled of untreated damp and ancient cooking—an unappetizing combination of mould, old vegetables, and fried onions. The creeping patch of black mould had returned to the ceiling in the corner nearest the back door, and the pile of newspapers meant for recycling was weeks old. There were crumbs on the table along with a pile of unanswered mail and three dirty cups, a bath-towel draped across one of the chairs, and an odd sock on the floor. When I'd left, the general dirt and untidiness had been invisibly familiar, but now I saw it as a stranger might, and was dismayed. The very thought of all that needed to be done made me tired.

I couldn't cope with it now. Without even pausing to make a cup of tea, I dumped my bag in the bedroom and escaped upstairs to the loft-conversion that was my office. There it was untidy, but not noticeably unclean, and the air was filled with the friendly familiar smell of old books. I picked my way through the stacks on the floor to my desk, where I switched on the computer and went straight to my email inbox.

Selwyn, bless him, was already on the case, but along with the rousing words of his faith in my ability to write a "splendid, uniquely insightful biography" of Helen Ralston, his

email carried disquieting news. He'd found an article—
"Masks and Identity in Three American Novels"—published
three years earlier in an academic journal. The author, Lilith
Fischler, Tulane University, was said to be working on a book
about Helen Elizabeth Ralston.

> This should certainly be taken with a grain of salt
> [he wrote]—academics are required to be always
> working on some project or other, and very few of
> these putative books ever appear in print. And if it
> does exist it is more likely to be a critical study than
> a biography. But why don't you ask her and find out?

The prospect scared me right out of the office and back
downstairs, where I began to clean the kitchen. As I scrubbed
and washed and tidied, I brooded about what to do.

I must write to her, of course. But what should I say? How
much should I tell her? How could I get her on my side?

My usual inclination when writing to strangers is to keep
the letter short and formal, but I knew that this could back-
fire. I could come across as cold when I only meant to be
unobtrusive, and, in an email, particularly, it was treacher-
ously easy to be misunderstood. What if Lilith Fischler read
my formality as arrogance? I didn't want to alienate her;
with a little effort maybe she'd be glad to help. Writing this
letter required almost as much care as composing a book
proposal to send to an unknown editor.

I considered my approach very carefully, balancing and
polishing phrases as I scrubbed the kitchen surfaces. By the
time I had the room spruced up, the letter was ready in my
head. I ate a sandwich, and went upstairs to write to the
address Selwyn had provided.

Next I went looking for my copy of *In Troy*. It wasn't on the shelf where I'd remembered it, so I searched all the bookcases, and then, very carefully, investigated every stack and corner of my office. I didn't remember lending it to anyone, so it was probably in one of the boxes in the loft, where the only way to find a particular book was to crouch down with a flashlight in the dark, and dig.

Instead, I went online to see what I could find out about Helen Ralston.

My first trawl didn't net much, but I was able to find copies of her second and fifth novels, as well as one of the many reprints of *Hermine in Cloud-Land* available to order. Two first editions of *In Troy* were listed: the dealer in London was asking $452.82 while one in San Francisco offered a lovingly-described "very fine" copy for a mere $320.00. There were also lots of the Virago edition about, with the cheapest offered at $2.00. On a whim, I added that to my order.

Before I logged off I checked my email again and found that Lilith Fischler had already replied.

My efforts had paid off. Her reply was as transparently open and friendly as I had struggled to make mine seem, and she told me exactly what I had been hoping to hear. She was *not* writing a biography, only a critical study of *In Troy*. Her essay would be appearing in an anthology to be published by Wesleyan University Press next year—she'd be happy to send me a copy as a file attachment. More importantly, she knew how to get in touch with Helen Ralston:

> She was happy to talk about her writing, but not so much about her early life, and especially not about the relationship with W. E. Logan. But she sent very

clear and interesting answers to everything else. I don't know if she will be quite as energetic and coherent now, since she had a stroke last year. Her daughter, Clarissa Breen, wrote to me that she was recovering well, but couldn't live on her own anymore. They sold the flat in London, and Helen is now living with Clarissa in Glasgow. I'm sure she wouldn't mind me giving you the phone number...

At nine o'clock the next morning, I rang the number Lilith Fischler had given me and asked the woman who answered if I could speak to Helen Ralston.

"May I ask who's calling?"

I gave my name, adding quickly, "She doesn't know me; I'm a writer. I wanted to talk to her about her work."

"Hold on a minute, I'll just get her."

Much more than a minute passed before the phone was picked up again, and I heard the same woman's voice saying, "I'm sorry, she doesn't want to speak on the phone; can you come here?"

I was so startled I could hardly speak at first. I'd assumed that this invitation would come much later, if at all. I finally managed to say, "Of course. If you'll give me directions. But I'm quite a distance away—in Argyll, on the west coast. It'll take me a couple of hours to drive to Glasgow."

"Ah. Well, tomorrow would be better, then. She's at her best in the mornings; she flags a bit around mid-day."

"I could come tomorrow. Whatever time suits you."

"Nine o'clock?"

"I'll be there."

"Thank you," she said warmly, surprising me. "I know mother is looking forward to meeting you. She doesn't have much excitement in her life these days—it was a real blow to her to have to leave London. The mention of your name perked her right up."

"That's nice," I said, surprised that my name should mean anything to Helen Ralston. "Can you tell me how to get to your house?"

"Do you know Glasgow at all? Well, it's not difficult, if you come in on the Great Western Road . . ."

HELEN Ralston lived with her daughter in an ordinary two-storey, semi-detached house in a quiet neighborhood on the northwestern edge of the city. The drive through Argyll, along the narrow, loch-hugging road, switching back upon itself again and again as it crossed a land divided and defined by water, up into the mountains and then down again, went more swiftly than I'd dared to hope, without any of the delays that could be caused by log-lorries, farm vehicles, and road works, and I was parking on the street in front of the house at five minutes after nine o'clock the following morning. I got out of the car stiffly, feeling numb and a little dazed by the speed of it all. That so soon after deciding I wanted to write about Helen Ralston I should be meeting her seemed little short of miraculous.

Her picture *My Death* was in the boot of the car, well-wrapped, ready to be handed back to its rightful owner, yet now that I was here in front of her house, I hesitated. Remembering my first, visceral reaction to it, I could not expect that the artist's reaction would be the ordinary one of someone to whom a piece of lost property has been returned. What if she was angry that I'd seen it? I decided to wait and see, try to find out her likely response before admitting that I had it.

That settled, I opened the side door to take out my bag and hesitated again at the sight of my new tape recorder, bought yesterday in the Woolworths in Oban.

I was unprepared for this interview in more ways than one.

Yesterday, I had discovered that my cassette recorder, which had seen me through more than ten years of occasional interviewing, was no longer working. I'd driven off to Oban immediately to buy one, only to find that the electronics shop I'd remembered had closed down—driven out of business, I guessed, by the stacks of cut-price VCRs, DVD players, printers, personal stereos, and telephones on sale in the aisles of Tesco. Alas for me, Tesco did not sell cassette recorders—players, yes, but nothing with a recording function. The closest equivalent I'd been able to find after searching every store in town was a toy for young children. It was the size of a school lunch-box and made of bright red and yellow plastic, with a bright blue microphone attached to it by a curly yellow cord. But it worked, and so I'd bought it.

Now, though, I knew I couldn't possibly arrive for my first meeting with Helen Elizabeth Ralston clutching this children's toy. In any case, she hadn't agreed to an interview; I hadn't even spoken to her yet. I couldn't remember if I'd told her daughter that I was planning to write a biography, but I was pretty sure I'd said only that I admired her mother's work and wanted to talk to her about it. Best if this first meeting should be informal, relaxed, a friendly conversation. Questions "for the record" could come later.

With some relief, I left the childish machine in the car and locked the door behind me. Now my dissatisfaction with the few questions I'd been able to formulate no longer mattered, no more than the fact that I could barely remember anything about *In Troy* (I'd spent a fruitless hour searching the loft for it) and hadn't yet even seen any of her other books. We were just going to talk.

From the first moment I saw her, I knew I would like Clarissa Breen. Sometimes it happens like that: you seem to recognize someone you've never set eyes on before and feel drawn to them, as if you're both members of the same far-flung family. I don't know why it should be, but those instantaneous feelings are nearly always right.

I smiled at her, and she smiled back, and from the warmth and interest in her grey eyes I knew she felt the same about me.

She was a slight, trim woman who appeared to be about my own age, her light brown hair in a short, feathery cut. The only faintly whispered echo of Circe's features was in her deep-set, luminous eyes; her own face was softer, wider, friendlier, her chin and nose less prominent, and she had a lovely, long smiling mouth.

As I liked her, so I also felt immediately at home in her house. I liked the dramatic mauve color of the entrance hall, the atmospheric black and white photographs hanging on the wall opposite the stairs, the scent of fresh coffee and something baking that wafted through from the back of the house.

The room to which she led me was a combination of kitchen and living room. At one end, a wicker couch was set into a window recess, grouped together with a glass-topped table and a couple of arm chairs. My eyes were briefly distracted by the green of the garden beyond the window, where birds hopped and hovered around a bird-table, and then I caught sight of the shriveled, white-haired figure hunched in a chair, and my heart gave a great, frightened leap.

"Mum, here's someone come to see you."

Feeling horribly self-conscious, more awkward than I had since the first few interviews I'd done for a student newspaper, I went forward on legs that felt like sticks of wood. Bending down to her, speaking in a voice that struck my own ears as harsh and unnatural, I introduced myself and began to explain my interest. I hadn't got very far before she interrupted.

"I know who you are," she said sharply, blinking watery blue eyes. "I was wondering when you'd finally get here."

Although I felt intimidated, I said, "I left home before seven. I think I made pretty good time."

The old lady made an impatient huffing sound and stretched out an arm. "That's not what I meant. Never mind. I suppose we should say how do you do."

Awkward still, and wishing that my heart would stop racing, I took her skinny, age-spotted hand gently in mine. "I'm very pleased to meet you. Thank you so much for letting me come."

"You're younger than I thought you'd be. I suppose you think you're old."

I smiled uncertainly. "I think I'm middle-aged, although that's right only if I live to a hundred."

She made a little sound, half sniff, half grunt. "Well, sit down," she said. "I suppose you'll want to ask me questions about my life?"

Clarissa came over with a tray. "Coffee all right for you? Mum, do you want anything else?" She turned to me. "I'll be in my office, down the hall, first door on the right—just come and knock if you need anything, but I'm sure Mum will look after you."

I felt sorry to see her go.

"Like her?"

Helen's question startled me. "She seems very nice."

"She is. She's a wonderful daughter, but, more than that, I think we'd be friends even if we weren't related."

"That must be nice, to feel like that. To have that sort of relationship." I waited tensely for the inevitable next question, but it didn't come.

"Yes. It is."

I took a sip of coffee, then put the cup down and rummaged in my bag for notepad and pen. "I thought . . . do you mind if I take a few notes? Or, or would you rather we just talked, and I could record a more formal interview later?"

"It's up to you. Why ask me? Surely you've done this sort of thing before." She sounded disapproving, and I didn't blame her. I didn't understand myself what had thrown me into such a flutter, as if I were a kid again, the novice reporter speechless before her first visiting celebrity. I'd interviewed more than a hundred people, most of them more famous than Helen Elizabeth Ralston. But this was different, not only because this wasn't an assignment—there was no newspaper behind me, I didn't even have a contract for a book—but because it was *her*. She mattered so much; I wanted her to like me; I wanted to be friends with the author of *In Troy*.

And I knew that if I wanted to prove myself to her, I was going about it in exactly the wrong way.

"I want you to be comfortable," I said, as firmly as I could. "I did think that we might start by chatting—I'll bring a recorder next time—and if there's anything you don't want to talk about . . ."

"I'll let you know."

"OK, then." I took a deep breath and took the plunge. "What made you, an American, decide to come to Glasgow to study art?"

She peered at me. "Right to the heart of it? All right, let's get this over with. It was for W. E. Logan."

"You knew his work?"

"I had seen one painting, a landscape. One of my teachers, the head of the art department at Syracuse, owned it. He had met Logan and some other Scottish painters on a visit to the South of France a few years earlier, and been very impressed by his work... although not, I think, quite as greatly impressed by it as I was. I don't know, young people, they're so wild, so ready to fly off at the slightest encouragement, don't you think?" She shot me a little, conspiratorial smile. "Well, I was, anyway. I must have been searching for a mentor, as young people often do. At any rate, soon after seeing this picture, which I convinced myself was a masterpiece, I wrote off to the artist, Mr Logan, in far-away Scotland, and I sent him some of my sketches, and I asked for his comments and advice.

"And his advice—now, you may find this hard to believe, but I still have the letter; I've kept it all these years, and I'll let you see it later—his response was to praise my work to the skies and tell me that the next step was to find the right teacher and embark on a proper course of study. Despite my living so far away—had he even noticed where the letter came from?—the school that he recommended was his own, where he could be my teacher. At that age, and in my impressionable state of mind, a suggestion from W. E. Logan had the force of a command."

She paused to pick up a glass of water from the table and take a small sip.

I was astonished. How was it that Logan's biographer hadn't known this? And why had Logan himself tried to cover it up, with his little fantasy about Helen's prophetic dreams? "I'd love to see your sketches from that time."

"They're gone."

"Oh, no! What happened?"

She lifted her narrow shoulders. "I don't know what became of them. They're long gone. I didn't take them with me when I left Glasgow. I suppose Willy—or his wife—might have destroyed them."

It was on the tip of my tongue to tell her about the painting in the car. "Maybe not all of them."

She shrugged. "They're nothing to me now. And they weren't then, or I would have kept them, wouldn't I."

"Like you kept W. E. Logan's letter to you."

"Letters. There were several, tucked inside my diary. I took that with me to Paris."

"*Paris*? You left Glasgow for Paris? Why?"

Her smile this time included her eyes, which narrowed so much they nearly disappeared. "Why Paris?" she repeated slowly. "My dear, it was 1929. I was an artist, I was an American, cut loose, without much money but free—where would *you* have gone?"

I met her eyes and smiled back. "Paris," I agreed. "Of all the places and times I wish I could see for myself—Paris, in the twenties."

"Well, then. You understand."

"Tell me—what was it like? What did you do there? Did you know anyone?"

She raised her eyebrows and looked away. "So many questions! My, my. Where to begin?" She reached with a hand that trembled slightly for her water glass. I waited until she had taken another tiny sip and put the glass back down before I repeated, "Did you know anyone in Paris when you arrived?"

"No. Not personally. But I knew a few names, and it was

not hard, then, to fall in with the expatriate crowd. There were certain cafés and hotels where they gathered. And, as a young woman, unaccompanied, reasonably attractive, it was easy to make new friends."

FOR THE next hour Helen Ralston kept me entranced and fascinated with anecdotes from her years in Paris. She name-dropped without restraint. I could hardly believe my luck, to be sitting in the same room, talking to someone who had actually attended some of Gertrude Stein's famous salons. Picasso and Hemingway were both, by then, *much* too grand to be known—she said—she'd seen them around, though. And she'd been friendly with Djuna Barnes and Man Ray and Marcel Duchamp and Brancusi, Caresse and Harry Crosby, Anaïs Nin and Henry Miller, and she'd taken tea with Sylvia Beach and James Joyce and his Nora...so many evocative names.

At one point I remember thinking *She's a living time machine*, and at another I could have cursed myself for not having brought in the tape recorder, however idiotic it looked. How could I remember all the details? Would she be willing to relate all these stories again another day? It occurred to me that maybe there wouldn't *be* another interview—not that she'd be unwilling to talk to me again, but simply because she could drop dead at any minute. At her age, especially, you couldn't count on anything.

I wanted her to go on talking forever, to soak up as much of her remembered experiences as I possibly could, but after a couple of hours it was clear she was running out of energy.

The pauses for tiny sips of water became more frequent, and her face seemed to sag, and she stumbled often over simple words. Even aware of this, I was too selfish to let her stop; it was only when Clarissa came in and exclaimed at the sight of her mother's obvious exhaustion that Helen finally fell silent.

"Time for a break," said Clarissa.

I jumped up guiltily. "I'm sorry, I've just been so fascinated—"

"I'm all right, I'm all right," Helen said, flapping a hand at her daughter. "Don't *fuss*."

"You're tired—"

"Yes, of course I'm tired—what's wrong with that? It means I'll sleep. I'll have my rest now, and eat later."

I chewed my lip, watching as Clarissa helped her mother rise from the chair.

"I'm fine, I'm fine, don't fuss me."

"I'll just come upstairs and see you into bed. Excuse us," Clarissa said as she and her mother moved slowly across the room.

When they had gone out, I wandered aimlessly around the room, gazing out the window at the birds and then looking around at the pictures on the walls—they were highly-detailed drawings of plants, like illustrations from an old-fashioned botany book. I had noticed a bookcase in one corner, and now gravitated towards it. A few familiar spines caught my attention immediately—*Nightwood, The Rings of Saturn, Hallucinating Foucault, Possession*—all dear friends which I had at home—and then the breath caught in my throat at the sight of a familiar pink and blue spine, the letters of my own name written there above the title. I had to put my hand on it and draw it out, and yes, it was one of my own short story collections.

I was still holding it, bemused and pleased, when Clarissa came back in.

"Out like a light," she said.

"I'm sorry—"

"Oh, that's all right, she loved it! But she can't take much excitement, that's all. Sad when talking about the past is the most excitement you can know." She noticed the book in my hands then and gave me a different sort of smile. "I liked your stories. I didn't think I would—I don't read sci-fi or fantasy—but yours aren't really sci-fi, are they? They're more like myths. I especially liked that one where the mother is born again—what's it called?—where she becomes a little baby, and her son has to look after her."

"Thank you." Always nice to meet a reader, but I couldn't help the quick stab of disappointment. "I thought maybe this belonged to Helen."

"Of course it does. She has all your books. That's just the only one I've read—but now I'll be sure to read the others," she said quickly.

"Helen Ralston has read all my books?" This was better than winning an award.

"Of course. Why do you suppose she was so excited to meet you? Didn't she tell you?"

"The conversation didn't go in that direction."

Clarissa shrugged and rolled her eyes. "Well. Would you like another coffee? There's a pastry in the oven. Mum has a sweet tooth, and normally I take a break and join her about now." As she spoke, we had been drifting together towards the kitchen area, where she now took a cinnamon plait from the oven.

"What sort of work do you do?" I asked.

"Writing—but not like yours or Mum's. It's mostly catalogue

copy and travel brochures. I used to work in marketing. This is handy because I can do it from home."

We settled in against the counter, sipping coffee and nibbling the warm, sweet, soft pastry while we traded information about our lives, laying the foundations for a friendship. After about a quarter of an hour, her eyes strayed to the clock on the stove, and although I wanted nothing more than to go on talking to Clarissa, I knew I was interrupting her work, so I said, "I should be going."

"You're welcome to stay," she said, hesitating slightly. "If you wanted to wait and say goodbye to Mum when she wakes up . . . only I don't think she'll have the energy for much more than that."

"No, that's all right, as long as I can come back—how about the day after tomorrow? If that's not too soon?"

"That should be fine. I'll call you if there's any problem. I've got your number."

As soon as I got back to the car, I remembered *My Death* still in the boot. I thought of taking it up to the house and handing it over to Clarissa, just to get the problem off my hands, but then decided that wasn't fair. I'd make a point of mentioning it to Helen next time. I felt I could count on getting a fairly rational response, although whether she'd be happy to have this strange painting back in her possession again, I didn't know.

Before starting on the long drive home, I went shopping. I bought myself a neat, unobtrusive mini-cassette recorder and spent some more time in the bookshops of Glasgow, this time concentrating on memoirs and histories of Paris in the 1920s and 1930s, searching for and finding Helen Ralston's name in index after index.

The next day, two of the books I had ordered—*Hermine*

in Cloud-Land and *The Second Wife*—arrived in the post, so the time passed pleasurably in reading. I was not very impressed by Willy Logan's first book. The pictures were charming, but by comparison the text strained after charm and achieved only a kind of dated, fey whimsicality. I didn't care for it and, having met the original of Hermine, I didn't think that she would have either.

The Second Wife, Helen Ralston's fifth novel, was a revelation: understated, subtle, psychologically complex, ambiguous, and faintly sinister...it was just the sort of novel I aspired to write myself, and reading it now, at this fallow period of my life, stirred a creative envy in me. For the first time in ages I wished I was at work on a novel and, although I knew I wasn't anywhere near ready to start one, I could believe that one day I would be, that the roads of fiction weren't forever closed to me. Maybe, after I'd finished with Helen Ralston, I'd be inspired by her example to write fiction again.

That night, the unseasonably dry, mild weather broke, and a gale began to blow. I lay awake listening to the keening wind, the rain flung like shot against the windows, and worried. I hated driving in bad weather; I was nervous enough about the narrow, twisting roads in this country when they were dry and the visibility was good—had it been anyone else I was going to meet, I would have phoned to suggest rescheduling. But at Helen Ralston's age, any day might be her last. I felt I had to go.

By six o'clock in the morning the winds had died; but the rain had settled in, falling heavily and relentlessly from the laden sky. A few hours of that, and the road I lived on would be flooded, impassable. I made a thermos of coffee and a peanut butter sandwich to take in the car along with my heavy-weather gear, a flashlight, and the shoulder bag holding

The Second Wife, notebook, new tape recorder, extra batteries and tapes, and drove off without giving myself time to reconsider. *My Death* was still in its wrappings in the boot, awaiting delivery.

I was tense and cautious, and although the rain had scarcely lessened by the time I reached the outskirts of Glasgow and the traffic reports on Radio Scotland warned of problems on other roads, my way was clear. Drawing up in front of Clarissa Breen's house I felt the happy relief of the traveller who has, against all odds, battled safely home again.

"Home is the sailor, home from sea," I murmured to myself as I hurried up the walkway. Clarissa, opening the door to my knock, looked surprised and pleased.

"I thought we'd be getting a call from you to say you weren't going to risk it—this rain is dreadful!" she exclaimed, letting me in.

There was the same smell of coffee and something sweet baking, and the black and white photographs displayed against the mauve walls of the entrance hall looked as familiar as if I'd been coming in through that front door for months. I sighed happily. "Oh, the roads weren't bad, really. How are you? How's Helen?"

I had not spoken loudly, but my voice must have carried to the back of the house, because the old woman shouted, "Waiting for you so we can get started!"

"Very bright today," said Clarissa, behind me, and murmured closer to my ear, "A little overexcited."

"Tears before bed-time?"

"Let's hope not."

"What are you *talking* about out there? She's *my* visitor, Clarissa! Let her come through, don't you keep her gossiping!"

We exchanged a glance, and I was split between enjoying

our conspiracy and guilt over betraying Helen, and then I went on ahead into the big, bright room.

"Hello, Helen. It's good to see you again. How are you?"

"Not getting any younger," she said crisply. Her eyes were sparkling; she looked pleased with herself. "You see, Clarissa, didn't I say she would come? I knew she wouldn't be scared of rain!"

"I couldn't live in Scotland if I were."

I was soon settled into a chair beside Helen, with a cup of fresh, strong, hot coffee close at hand and my unobtrusive little tape recorder pointing in her direction.

"I thought we might talk a bit about your childhood," I said. I had decided to be organized and chronological about my investigations, even though, after reading *The Second Wife*, I longed to talk about that.

A small sigh escaped her, and I felt I'd disappointed her in some way. "Very well. Ask your questions."

"Well . . . do you want to start by telling me your earliest memory?"

She looked vague. "I can try. Mostly what I remember are *things*, not events, so it's hard to put a time to them. The first house where I lived, where I was born—we were there until I was about eleven—all my memories are there. I could close my eyes now and take you on a tour of that house, describing every room, all the furniture, every nook and cranny, not just how it looked from every perspective, but the texture of the rugs and the painted walls and the bathroom tiles, the smells and tastes as well—but that would be far too boring."

I felt my heart beat faster in sympathy. In fact, this was exactly how I felt about my own first childhood home, which remained more clear in my memory, more *real*, than anywhere I had lived since. Those first ten years of life, in which I had so exhaustively explored my surroundings, had given me a depth of useless knowledge, made me an expert in the geography and furnishings of the house at 4534 Waring Street, Houston, Texas, between the years 1952 and 1963. I supposed that other people—unless, like my first husband, they'd moved house every year or two—carried around with them a similarly useless mental floorplan and inventory—but until now I'd never heard anyone else talk about it.

"I remember, there was colored glass in the window, a fanlight, above the front door, and when the sun shone through it made a pattern of magical, shimmering colors against the wall. I remember trying to touch the colors, to catch them, and feeling frustrated that they slipped through my fingers—I was too young to understand.

"And there was a wonderful old, dark wood chest that I was always trying to get into. It didn't matter how many times I saw inside, that it was only blankets and linens and so on, I would still imagine it was hiding some treasure. That was one of my fancies . . . my dreams and my fancies, now, I remember some of them as clearly as the things that were real. Perhaps my earliest memory was a dream.

"I had a toy. It might have been my first toy, maybe my only one—children didn't have so many toys in those days, you know, we made do with bits and pieces, cast-off things our elders had no use for, a wooden spoon with a face for a doll, but this was a ready-made toy, it had been manufactured for no other purpose but play. It was a doll made of rubber, an ugly little thing really I suppose, but it was my baby and I loved it dearly. Sometimes I'd put my finger into its mouth to let it suck—because its mouth would open if you squeezed it, and close again when the pressure was released—and sometimes I'd take its whole head into my mouth and suck on it—not very motherly behavior, but I wasn't much more than a baby myself, and perhaps I resented having been weaned—at any rate, I wanted something to suck. Once I bit off a piece of its nose—something about the color and the texture of it convinced me it would taste nice, but of course it didn't; it tasted of rubber, nasty, although the sensation of chewing it, feeling it slide through my teeth and then catch, again and again, was intriguing enough that I was in no hurry to spit it out. After I'd chewed a hole in it, of course the doll no longer worked properly, the mouth wouldn't open and shut like before, but that didn't bother me, I still loved it and carried it around with me everywhere until one day I suppose I must have dropped it when I was out, and my mother didn't pick it up, and so I lost my baby, my treasure, my first child, you might say."

She looked at me as if expecting some comment, but I could not respond. I felt almost giddy with *déjà vu*—only this wasn't merely *déjà vu,* but something much stronger and stranger, and it had cut the ground right out from under me. I didn't know what to think about what I was hearing: could it be coincidence? Lots of children in the past century must have owned rubber dolls and sucked and chewed them to destruction. She hadn't even described it very well—my doll had been a sort of clown, but hers presumably was a baby.

When I said nothing, she went on.

"I don't remember when I lost it, how it happened, when I noticed, if I was upset, and I don't know how long after that it was that he came back to me in a dream."

I noticed the switch from "it" to "he," and saw my own long-lost clown doll in my mind's eye.

"It wasn't a detailed dream, it was just him. He had come back. But instead of being glad to see him, I was frightened, and I screamed and woke myself up. I woke the whole house up with my screaming.

"When I told my mother about it I began to cry. She thought I was unhappy because I missed my doll. She didn't understand. To have the doll back was the last thing I wanted. I was terrified in case I did by some chance find it again, because I knew... I knew it would be like the dream. He would have changed. He wouldn't be my baby anymore. What the dream had shown me was the familiar become strange, how frightening the ordinary can be. You understand?"

I stared back as if hypnotized and just managed to nod my head. But I didn't understand. How could this person—a stranger, and of another generation—have had the very same dream as me? Even her interpretation, although different from my own, rang true, so that I thought yes, that was the real reason my dream had scared me.

As I still said nothing, after another little pause, Helen went on talking about her childhood. I hardly listened. I was in a welter, all confused, of frightening emotions as I tried to make sense of this impossible connection between us. I could not accept that it was mere coincidence, that *both* of us had shared the same experience as children—an experience that had given rise to the same dream, which had been significant enough for both of us to remember it all our lives. There had to be a reason for it; some link, an explanation...

And suddenly I remembered what I had, of course, known all along. That dream of mine, that highly significant, personal memory, was no secret. I had written about it. I had put it into a short story that anyone could read—I knew that both Clarissa and Helen had read it, because it was in the volume I'd found in their bookcase.

But what did Helen mean by telling me back my own

story as if it were one of her own memories? Was it a joke? A tease? A veiled compliment?

At any rate, unless she was genuinely senile, confused enough that she couldn't sort out her own experiences from things she'd only read about, she must have expected me to recognize what she was doing, and comment on it. I recalled her suggestive pauses, the way she had looked at me and awaited a response, and I almost groaned aloud.

What an idiot she must think me!

Maybe she was feeling foolish herself, knowing her joke had misfired, thinking, perhaps, that my dream was not real, but something I'd made up, a passing notion that meant so little to me that I'd forgotten it and took her "memory" at face value.

I couldn't say anything now—she'd reached high school in her recollections, and it would be far too rude to interrupt her to say that I'd belatedly got her joke—I'd have to wait until she gave me an opening.

Maybe it was because I was concentrating so hard on not missing my chance to speak, but I could not get involved in what she was telling me. It seemed remote and unreal, second-hand, as if she was just retelling a tale she had memorized. Maybe that was my fault: perhaps she felt it was her duty, to get things right and in the proper sequence, and had prepared this potted history for me. But I missed the lively, spontaneous jumble of impressions that had come bubbling up the day before when she'd talked about her years in Paris.

We had soon reached the point where the young Helen Ralston made her dramatic, life-changing decision to leave America and go to study art in Glasgow.

"But you know all that," she said briskly. "And I've told you about Paris..."

"Wait, wait." I held up a hand. "Slow down and back up. You *didn't* tell me about your time in Glasgow—not at all. I sort of understand why you went, but not really—"

"What do you mean 'not really'? I told you, it was because of his letters. I suppose I fell in love with him. Well, it wouldn't be the first time such a thing has happened. I still have those letters, you know! I can show you."

"I'm not doubting you," I said quickly. "But what happened after you got to Glasgow—you haven't told me any of that."

She gave me a long, hooded look—very like a bird of prey considering whether it was worthwhile to pounce—before she spoke. "But you know, don't you." It was hardly a question.

"I've read one side of the story. I'd really like to hear yours."

"I don't know why. I'm sure you can imagine it well enough. Why is it people are only interested in women because of their connections to some man, some famous man?"

"That's not true."

She wasn't listening to me. "The letters I've had from people wanting to know *the truth*! That's what they say, but it isn't the truth they want at all, just gossip. Did Helen Ralston try to kill herself because Willy Logan wouldn't stay with her, or was she trying to get away from him? Or was it nothing to do with him at all, and he only happened to be there? Something happened—it happened more than seventy years ago—does it matter *why* it happened?"

"It matters to me—*your* story is the one I want to hear."

Her eyes flickered. "Then why keep asking about Logan?"

"I'm not—I don't mean to. I want to know what happened to you. How you felt about things. Everything. Your childhood, your youth, the time you spent in Glasgow and Paris, and everything else. I know you weren't with Logan for long.

Not even two years. Out of ninety-six years, that's not much. But it is a part of your life—the things that happened to you in your early twenties—"

"The truth."

I shut up.

She leaned forward, fixing me with her deep-set, faded blue eyes, her hands like claws clutching the chair arms. "The truth is that I don't know why Helen Ralston jumped out of that window—or if she was pushed. It happened to someone else. I don't remember anything about it."

I knew that serious accidents could sometimes result in memory loss, but I thought of the way she had given me back my own dream as if it were her own, and I wasn't sure I believed her.

"OK. But you mentioned a diary—"

"Yes, and I'll let you see it. You can see all of them, in due course."

"Thank you. That will be very helpful. And we'll leave that day in August. But—would you mind talking about something else that happened before you left Glasgow and W. E. Logan?"

She shrugged her shoulders slightly. "What is it you want to know?"

"About the island. Achlan. I wonder if you could tell me about that."

There was a sharp click, and we both looked at the tape recorder, which had switched itself off.

"It's OK," I said, reaching for it. "I've got another cassette in my bag."

"I'd like something to drink. My mouth is so dry."

I stood up. "Shall I get you some more water? Or something else?"

"Why don't you go fetch Clarissa, and we'll take our break now."

It was too early; we'd had barely an hour together, and I knew that after the break she'd be bound to go for a nap. My disappointment must have shown, because she gave a small, thin-lipped smile. "Oh, don't worry. We'll get back to the island. I promise you, we'll get back to Achlan."

Clarissa did not seem surprised when I knocked at her door.

"She was up at six this morning, rummaging through her papers, sorting things out, making notes, muttering to herself. Getting ready for you. Nearly bit my head off when I dared suggest you might not come today, because of the weather. 'Of course she'll come! She has to come!'"

Strangely, a shiver ran through me at the idea of the two of them talking about me in my absence, although there was surely nothing odd or sinister in it.

"Such a shame, when you've come such a long way for such a short visit...Tell you what, why don't you stay for lunch today, and talk to Mum again later on?"

"That would be wonderful—if she's up for it."

"I'm sure she'll tell you if she's not." Clarissa grinned.

Over fresh coffee—decaffeinated for Helen—and slices of apple tart, talk about Helen's life went on, leap-frogging a couple of decades to London during the Blitz and the brief war-time love affair with Robbie, a much younger fighter pilot. He was Clarissa's father, although he'd not lived to see his only child. I was surprised to learn that Clarissa was sixty—I told her honestly that she looked much younger—but she'd been born during the war, to a grieving single mother.

"I named her after *Mrs Dalloway*," Helen informed me. "I was reading that book during my confinement—in fact,

I read it three times. It was the only escape I had, a window into the world before the War, London before the bombs fell, before . . ." she trailed off, blinking rapidly, and her daughter stroked her hand.

Helen's memories of the war years in London were vivid, her descriptions of that time of fear, tedium, deprivation, and passion full of the circumstantial detail I'd missed when she had talked about her earlier life. People said that when you got older the past seemed more immediate and was easier to recall than more recent years, but in every life there must also be periods you would rather forget, and others that you kept fresh by constantly reviewing. Obviously Helen had not wanted to lose a single, precious moment from her short time with Clarissa's father—from the way that Clarissa listened and smiled and chimed in, it was clear she'd heard it all before—but the affair with Willy Logan was different. Maybe it had been too unhappy, maybe her feelings and her actions then didn't suit her older self-image. I could well imagine her not wanting to remember what a reckless and troubled young girl she had been, whether she had seduced or been seduced by her teacher. In my experience, such an affair at such an age was too intense and life-shaping to be forgotten, but if anything could wipe the slate clean, I thought, it had to be a near-death experience.

Although Helen announced her intention that we should carry on talking, her energy was clearly flagging, so I chimed in with her daughter to insist that she have a lie down.

"I'll stay," I promised her. "Clarissa's invited me for lunch. I'll read while you're resting. We can talk all afternoon if you're up to it. I've brought plenty of cassettes."

Helen accepted this. "Come upstairs with me. I'll give you something to read. I'll show you those letters."

Clarissa went back to her work while I went slowly upstairs after Helen.

"I've kept diaries," she told me after she had paused to catch her breath at the top of the stairs. "And there's an autobiographical novel. I never wanted it published, before, but now, maybe . . . You could let me know what you think."

Her room was a dim, narrow space—an ordinary bedroom whose dimensions had been shrunk by the addition of bookshelves on every wall. There was one window, shaded and curtained. The shelves were deep, double-stacked with books, notebooks, and box-files. The other furnishings were a single bed, a small wardrobe, a bedside table, and something that might have been either a writing desk or a dressing table, but it was so cluttered with a mix of toiletries, papers, medicines, notebooks, tissues, books, and pens that it seemed unlikely it was used for either purpose now.

"My memories," said Helen. "We got rid of a lot when I moved up from London, but I had to keep my favorite books and all my papers." With a heavy sigh, she sank down onto the bed. Then, with a groan, she struggled to rise again. "My diaries. I was going to show you . . ."

I put a hand on her shoulder, pushing her gently down again. "I'll get it. Tell me where to look."

"Thank you, dear. If you don't mind . . ." She lay back, putting her head down on the pillow with a sigh of relief. "They're on my work-table. Desk. The whole lot. You're not ready to read them all, not yet, but you could look at one now, I think. Well, why not? Let me think. Which one? Hmmm."

Her eyes closed. I watched her uncertainly, feeling a mixture of affection, amusement, and exasperation as I realized she was falling asleep. I opened my mouth to call her back, but just then she gave a tiny, stuttering snore.

I turned to look at the table and saw the pile of notebooks she must have meant. She had been intending to give me one to read. I picked up the one on top, a hardbound black and red book with lined pages. There was nothing marked on the cover to indicate its contents. I opened it to the first page, a fly-leaf where she had written her name and the year, 1981. Oh, far too late.

I put the notebook down carefully to one side and reached for the next in the stack. This one was much more battered and obviously old. It had a blue and white marbled cover with a square in the centre of the front cover where it said COMPOSITIONS. I'd had one just like it in high school in the late 1960s and had used it to record my most intimate feelings, all the daily emotional upheavals, the first stirrings of sexual interest—to my misery, unreciprocated. How I'd poured my heart out, the protestations of my elaborate and undying love for the golden Yale—sometimes, long ago as it was now, I could still remember the particular bittersweet flavor of that feeling, the ache of unrequited love. And then, in the same year—things happened so rapidly in youth—there had been the mutual attraction between me and Andy, and the pain of being unloved had been assuaged by passionate love-making in the back of borrowed cars. My descriptions of what we'd done must have verged on the pornographic— even now, the idea of someone else reading about my first love affair horrified me. I suppose it was the thought of the contents of my own, so similar-looking diary, that made me set this one aside without even opening it to check the date.

As I did so, I dislodged a stack of photographs lying on top of the next notebook; they slithered in a watery rush down the side of the notebook-tower.

Shooting a quick, nervous glance at the figure in the bed

behind me, making sure that she still slept, I gathered them up. They were all old, black and white snapshots of people, most of them posed in some outdoor location. They were identified on the backs with penciled dates, names, or initials.

LONDON 1941 ROBBIE

I recognized Helen, skirted and hatted amid pigeons at the base of some statue, holding on to the arm of a uniformed young man. As I peered into the distant grey shadows of his face, my heart gave a jolt: in the curve of his mouth and the line of his jaw I thought I could see a resemblance to Allan. The likeness to Clarissa was obvious, and it dawned on me that this was why I'd felt so immediately drawn to her. Her father looked a bit like Allan, and she reminded me of him, too.

I glanced quickly through the other pictures, usually able to pick out Helen by her distinctive looks. Some of the other figures were also familiar: Djuna Barnes, Peggy Guggenheim, James Joyce. I caught my breath. In an English garden Helen Ralston stood, beaming triumphantly beside a tall, shy, elegant, faintly bemused-looking woman. There was no need for me to turn over the photo to check the name written on the back—Virginia Woolf was unmistakable.

Brilliant! My heart pounded with excitement. I wondered if she'd let me use these pictures in my book and immediately knew the answer. Of course she would—why else had she sorted them out, if not to give to me? With so many well-known names to toss into my proposal, I felt the biography was a done deal. *Helen Elizabeth Ralston, The Forgotten Modernist.* As I gathered the pictures up and stacked them neatly, again my eyes turned greedily to the pile of old journals.

The one now on top was a slightly odd size, narrower than the contemporary standard, bound in some stiff black cloth, and as I reached out to touch it I somehow *knew* that this was one of her earliest notebooks, from her Paris years.

Without even pausing to question my right to do so, I picked the book up and opened it.

There was no date on the first page and, as I flipped through, I got the impression that it was one continuous narrative, for it wasn't broken down into entries like a diary. It seemed to be told in the first person, and there were long passages of description, but also conversations, set off with single quotes and dashes. Maybe this was the autobiographical novel she had mentioned?

Helen's handwriting was small, neat, and angular, but despite its regularity it was not easy to read—especially not in the dim light of her bedroom. I flipped ahead a few pages and moved a little closer to the covered window, trying to find something I could make sense of. I saw that, despite the cramped and careful handwriting, she used her notebooks the same way I did, writing on only one side of the page. (I wondered if she had continued this profligacy during the war, with paper rationing.) The blank sides weren't wasted; for me they provided a space for notes, second thoughts, later comments, trial runs at complicated sentences, reminders, lists of interesting words and of books I wanted to read, occasionally quotations from the books I was reading, or ideas for stories, and as I flipped through the book, concentrating now on the "other" pages, I could tell that Helen worked just like me.

These pages were easier to read since there was less on them. I managed to puzzle out a few quotations: there were lines from Baudelaire—his French followed by her rough translation—a paragraph from *The Golden Bowl* and two from *The Great Gatsby*. A list of British and American authors might have been one of my own "must read" lists, with the difference being that all of them were still alive in 1929. I wondered if she was reminding herself of books to look for, or people she wanted to meet.

The next list was something else. I read it again and again, trying to make some other sense of it than the personal meaning it had for me at first glance:

Yale
Andy
Ira
Mark
John
Jimmy
Patrick
John
Chas
Allan

Nine masculine forenames, one of them repeated twice. The names of the ten men I had loved.

How could Helen Ralston have known that?

She couldn't; it wasn't possible; not *all* of them. My husbands were a matter of public record, and plenty of people knew that I'd lived with a man called Mark for three years. Although my affair with Ira was ostensibly secret, I had dedicated my first book to him, and, invited to contribute to a magazine feature called "The First Time," I hadn't bothered to disguise Andy with a pseudonym. But Yale? Or the fact that I'd been involved with two different men called John? And *nobody* knew about Chas.

Could it be coincidence? Another writer, drawing up a

list of names for characters, stumbling so precisely on those most meaningful to me?

I couldn't believe it.

I saw stars and jags of light in front of my eyes as I carefully replaced that notebook with the others.

Somehow, I got out of that stuffy little room, filled with the sound of an old woman's shallow breathing, without bumping into anything or falling over, and made my way down the stairs. I was halfway to the front door, driven by terror, before I remembered that my bag with all my things, including my car keys, was still in the kitchen.

Although I desperately wanted to sneak away, I couldn't. I went back to the big room to fetch my things, and then, after a moment of concentrating on my breathing, knocked at Clarissa's door.

The sight of me took the smile off her face. "What's wrong? Is it Mum?"

"Your mother's fine, she was sleeping when I left her. I'm afraid I've got to go—something's come up—" Unable to think of a convincing lie, I patted my shoulder bag as if indicating the presence of a mobile phone.

Clarissa's expression relaxed, but still she frowned. "Oh, dear. I hope it's not anything—"

"Oh, no, no."

"You're so pale."

I tried to laugh. "Really? Well, it's nothing terrible, just—kind of crossed wires, complicated to explain, but I have to be back there this afternoon. So—if you'll apologize to your mother?"

"Sure. You'll come again?"

"Oh, of course." I turned away from her as I spoke. "I'll phone in the next few days to arrange a time . . ." I felt like crying. I had liked her so much, and now I wondered if her seeming friendliness was part of some Byzantine plot, if she'd somehow been helping her mother to gather information about me, if they were stalkers, or planning something… but what? And why?

I stopped at the Little Chef in Dumbarton, not because I was hungry, but because I realized I was in no fit state to drive. I needed to stop and think.

The café was soothingly anonymous and, so late on a weekday morning, almost empty. I ordered the all-day breakfast and coffee—although I felt jittery enough already—and got out my pen and notebook to write down the list again.

It was a list I thought only I could have made. These weren't the only lovers I'd had in my life—in fact, two fiancés were missing—but they were, to me, the most significant. Yale hadn't even been my lover, except in fantasy, and I wasn't sure there was anyone now alive who knew how I'd felt about him. I'd never told *anyone* about my two-week fling with the man I'd called Chas—which wasn't even his real name! Only I had called him Chas, the personal nickname adding another layer of secrecy and fantasy to the forbidden passion.

I wondered, as I dug into my eggs and bacon, if I'd ever written down this list of names I knew so well. Perhaps, one lonely night, on a piece of paper, or in a notebook that had later gone missing…? That might explain *how* she knew it, although not why she would have been driven to copy it down on a blank page in one of her old notebooks. Was it possible that she'd become obsessed with me? That she, or her daughter, had been spying on me for some strange psychological reasons of their own, eventually maneuvering me into the idea of the biography…

No, no, that just wasn't possible. There had been no outside influence—I had suggested Helen Ralston's name to Selwyn, not vice versa. Even if Alistair Reid and *My Death* could have been a plant, no one could have influenced, or predicted, the chain of thoughts that had led to my decision. If I'd had some other idea on the journey to Edinburgh, or if I'd decided to go shopping instead of look at pictures...

Another possibility, which I thought of as I pushed my varifocal specs up on my nose and frowned in a futile attempt to make out the headlines on a newspaper at the other side of the room, was that I hadn't seen what I thought I'd seen. It was not unheard of for me to misread a word or two even in the best conditions, and in the dim light of Helen's bedroom I might have read Dale as Yale, Ivo as Ira, and been fooled by that into imagining that a list of perfectly ordinary male names was something uniquely personal to me.

I'd written too many stories about people with weird obsessions. It did not follow that just because Helen had read my stories, she was obsessed with me.

By the time I'd finished eating I'd convinced myself there was a wholly rational, nonthreatening explanation for it all. Yet some fearful, pre-rational doubt must have remained, because although I wrote a note to Helen, apologizing for rushing off as I had done and promising to be in touch again soon, I did not suggest a date for our next meeting, and I was in no hurry to arrange anything.

For the next two weeks I didn't write or think about writing. Instead, I cleaned house. I had a major clear-out, giving my own piles and stacks of stale belongings the same treatment I'd forced myself to apply to Allan's things a year earlier. I burned and recycled box-load after box-load of paper, made donations to the charity shops in Oban, and invited a Glasgow bookseller to come up and make me an offer. It wasn't easy, getting rid of so much stuff—I had to steel myself to it. But this was the obvious and necessary first step towards a major life-change. If I was going to be moving, I didn't want to be laden down with clutter, paying to shift box after box of stale memories, books, clothes, and other stuff I had not used in years.

The rain had been short-lived; the weather that spring was magnificent. It was the warmest, driest March I could remember since I'd moved to Scotland, and I took a break from my chores indoors to work outside, sanding down and repainting the window-frames, clearing and cutting back the normally wild and overgrown garden, getting everything ready for the change that I felt sure was coming, although I did nothing to make it happen.

And then it was April, with blue skies, fresh winds, and a warm and welcoming sun that seemed to say it was already summer. One morning the telephone rang, and it was Clarissa Breen.

A great wash of guilt made me hunch down in my chair, as if she could see me, and my cheeks began to burn. "I'm sorry I haven't been in touch, I was meaning to call," I said, and came to a sudden halt, unable to think of an excuse for my silence.

"That's OK. Mum was pleased to get your note. I did wonder...is everything all right?"

I couldn't remember what I had said, or hinted, about my reason for rushing out of the house. "Yes, yes, I'm fine. Everything's fine. I've just been busy, you know."

"That's good. Look, I don't want to bother you if you're busy—"

"No, no, I didn't mean—it's good to hear from you. I'm glad you called."

"I just wanted to let you know—there's no pressure, and I'll understand if you're busy—but we're going to be in your part of the world this weekend."

This news was so unexpected that I didn't know how to respond. "Do you need a place to stay?"

"Oh, no! That's not why—I didn't mean—only, if you'd like to meet for coffee, or a meal, some time. We'll be staying at the Crinan Hotel."

"That's great—of course I want to see you! You must come here for dinner one night. How long are you staying? Have you made a lot of plans?" All at once I was eager to see them again.

"Just for the weekend. Three nights. I really can't take any more time off right now, but Mum has been so desperate to get back up there lately, and with the weather being so fine, for once, and the forecast good—well, the time seemed right. I haven't made any plans yet; there's just one thing Mum really wants to do. I thought I'd ask at the hotel after we arrive. They might know someone who could take us out sailing one day."

"I'll take you out." I didn't even stop to think, although my heart was pounding so hard, I knew this was no light promise. I'd already guessed where Helen would want me to take her.

"Really? You have a boat?"

"Yes. And I'm fully qualified to sail her, so you don't have to worry. I haven't been out since . . . I haven't been out yet this year, and the forecast is good, as you say. It'll be fun."

We arranged that I would meet them at their hotel at nine o'clock Saturday morning and go out for a sail. I would bring provisions for a picnic lunch.

After her call, I went straight out to the boatyard, to find out if *Daisy*, to whom I'd given no thought whatsoever in more than a year, was in any state to be taken out on the water in a mere two days' time.

Fortunately, the manager of the boatyard, Duncan Mac-Innes, who was the best friend Allan and I had made during our years in Scotland, had taken as good care of *Daisy* as if she'd been his own, doing everything Allan would have done (and a bit more) without needing to be told, or intruding on my grief.

With the arrival of spring and the approach of the Easter holidays, even our quiet little boatyard was all bustle and go as everything was made ready for the start of the tourist season.

When I set eyes on *Daisy* she was back in the water after her long winter's sleep, barnacles scraped, rigging and sails repaired, the engine recently serviced, all neat and tidy and absolutely ship-shape, ready to go at a moment's notice.

I turned a look of wonder on Duncan. He stared at the boat, not at me, and rubbed his chin. "I thought, if you were interested, I could lease her out this season. There's always a demand for a sweet little boat like this one, and it can be a good way to make extra money."

"Thanks, but I think I'm going to want her for myself." After Allan's death I had thought once about selling *Daisy*, but she had been so intimately a part of our marriage that I had been unable to go through with it, even though keeping a boat, even one that you *do* use, is, as they say, a hole in the ocean for throwing money in.

Now he looked at me, still rubbing his chin. "Oh, aye, but we mostly do short leases anyway. One or two weeks at a time. You could book her for when you wanted her for yourself, and the rest of the time, you get paid. There's the upkeep, of course, but you could pay me a commission and I'd take care of that, and the expenses would all come out of the rental fees. I handle three other boats like that. All you have to do is say the word, and I'll add *Daisy* to the list."

As he spoke, I thought that perhaps he had mentioned this to me before, but I had been too deep in grief to take it in. I maybe hadn't understood, and he would have been too diffident to persist. I saw immediately now how sensible it was and how useful it would be to have another source of income. I told him so, and agreed to a meeting early the next week to arrange the details and fill in the paperwork.

I went home and surprised myself by actually writing a book proposal. It was only three pages, and it hinted at more than it explained, but I thought it might pique an editor's interest. I sent it as an email attachment to Selwyn without agonizing further. The time for procrastinating and running away was over. I was going to write Helen Ralston's life.

SATURDAY morning was bright and dry, the sun warm and the winds westerly and not too stiff, a perfect day for a pleasant little sail down the coast. The sight of Helen and Clarissa waiting for me in the lobby when I entered the Crinan Hotel made my heart beat a little faster, partly with pleasure, partly with fear.

Helen Ralston fascinated me; she also frightened me.

If my feelings for Clarissa were uncomplicated, the emotions Helen aroused were anything but.

This time, I didn't run away. It would have been easy enough to go forward, smiling and falsely apologetic, to claim there was something wrong with my boat and offer to take them out for a drive instead. Clarissa, I knew, would be on my side—I sensed she wasn't thrilled with the prospect of taking a ninety-six-year-old woman onto the ocean in a small boat—and Helen's anger, annoyance, disappointment could all be weathered.

The whole sequence of events for a safe, dull, socially uncomfortable day flashed through my mind in a split-second. I had only to say the word to make it happen, but I did not.

I decided instead to confront my fear and the mystery at the heart of Helen Elizabeth Ralston, and when she announced that we were going to pay a visit to the isle of Achlan, although my heart gave a queasy lurch, I still did not back down.

"Oh, yes, Eilean nan Achlan. The island of lamentation. I have your painting of it—it's in the boot of the car. I brought it to give back to you."

The old woman looked at me with her hooded hawk's eyes, unreadable. "I don't want it. You keep it. It's yours now."

Clarissa was frowning. I thought she would ask what we were talking about—I was eager to explain, ready to get the painting out of its wrappings and show it to her—but she was following her own train of thought.

"Mum, we can't go there. It's an uninhabited island. There's nowhere to land. You told me yourself how you had to swim ashore—I hope you don't imagine we're going swimming today!"

"*You'll* get us ashore, won't you?" Helen put her cold, clawlike hand on my arm and gave me an appealing, almost flirtatious look with tilted head.

I spoke over Helen's head to her daughter. "There's a dinghy on board, a little inflatable. We can go ashore in that."

"There, you see?" Helen looked as triumphant as she had in that old photograph with Virginia Woolf. This was a woman who liked to have her way.

"I still think it sounds like too much trouble," Clarissa said, offering me another chance to back out. "It's up to you, of course."

I was as curious—and almost as eager—as Helen to visit Achlan.

"It's not far away, and it's somewhere I've always meant to go. We—Allan and I—always meant to go ashore and explore, but we never did. I think it was because it was so close, too close—once we were out in the boat we wanted more of a sail."

"Well, if you really don't mind," Clarissa sighed.

I looked at Helen. "I'd like to get a picture of you there, today. For my book."

"You mean *my* book, don't you?"

"That's what I said." I gave her a bland, mock-innocent smile, and she snorted delicately.

I could see she was happy. And why not? I felt happy, too. It was only Clarissa who looked a bit out of sorts.

"Do you sail?" I asked her.

She shook her head. "No, I'm sorry. Is that a problem?"

"No, of course not. I can sail *Daisy* single-handed." Despite my long absence from her, she seemed to welcome me, and the old skills came rushing back. It was all very easy and smooth, pulling away from the dock and putting slowly out of the busy harbor until I was able to cut the noisy engine. I felt my own spirit crackle and lift like the crisp white sails as we went gliding through the Sound of Jura.

There are treacherous waters there, whirlpools and rocks of legendary fame, but I knew my way and was going nowhere near the local Scylla and Charybdis. I had only a short and easy sail ahead of me, never very far from shore. As I breathed in the fresh salt air and eased *Daisy* along the familiar sea-lane, I imagined Allan close beside me, his hand resting lightly atop mine on the tiller. He had taught me to sail. I felt an unexpected ease in the thought. I still missed him badly, but the memory no longer crippled me with sorrow. I could take pleasure in the good memories, and there were many of them, so many aboard this little boat.

Helen murmured, "Allan would have loved this."

It was as if she'd spoken my own thought aloud. I whipped around to stare at her, deeply shocked, but she didn't even notice, staring out at the water.

I thought of the list in her journal, and I moistened dry lips to croak, "Who?"

She turned to give me one of her filmy, blue-eyed stares. "Your husband, dear."

"How did you . . . I didn't know you knew him."

"Oh, yes." She nodded. "I met him in London. This was years ago—before you were married to him. He worked for Collins at that time, I think. My agent introduced us at a party, I do remember that. I was very struck by him. A lovely young man, so kind, yet so witty. That combination is rare, you know. And he reminded me more than a little bit of— but never mind that."

This was plausible. Allan *had* worked for Collins in the 1970s, years before I had known him, and he'd been a stalwart of the publishing party scene. And it was not surprising that Helen Ralston should have been drawn to him, recalling the photograph of Clarissa's father.

"But—how did you know—"

"That he was a sailor? We talked about it, of course! He told me about his holidays with his family, when he was a child, and how he learned to sail in the very same place where I came on holiday with Logan."

What I'd meant was how had she known that the man she'd met once, thirty years ago, had been my husband, but I realized there was no point in asking her. She might have claimed that I'd told her, or maybe she'd read it on a book-jacket. Anyone might have told her; it wouldn't have taken much effort to find out.

Plausible though her story of meeting Allan was, I didn't believe it. Allan had a wonderful memory for the people he'd met over the years, and he knew how much I loved *In Troy*. If he had ever met its author, he would have told me.

I was sure that Helen was teasing, just as she had been with the story of "her" dream, and that I would find out why before too much longer.

Eilean nan Achlan came into view within a few minutes, but I waited until we were much closer before pointing it out. Clarissa shaded her eyes with a hand to look. Helen turned her head with no change of expression.

"Did you ever come back?" I asked her.

She shook her head. "Never. I didn't want to, until now."

I steered *Daisy* into the little bay at the south-westerly end of the island and after some finicky maneuvering, hove to. I had judged it very well, I thought: the view from here was just about exactly what Helen Ralston had been looking at when she'd painted *My Death* more than seventy years before.

When I got a chance to rest after hauling in the sails and making everything tight, I looked at Helen to see how she was responding.

She was sitting very still, staring up at the gorse- and bracken-covered hills. Feeling my gaze upon her, she turned to meet my eyes. "Thank you," she said quietly. Something about her look or her tone sent a shiver down my spine.

"You're welcome. Shall we go ashore?"

"Yes. Let's."

Clarissa fought one last-ditch effort, casting an uneasy eye on the little rubber dinghy. "You know, I really don't think that's such a good idea, Mum . . ."

"Then you can stay here."

"That's not what I meant."

"I know. You meant that I should sit down and shut up like a good little girl. I'm not your child, Clarissa."

"No, but you do act like one sometimes!"

"It's my right."

"Why won't you be sensible!"

The two women glared at each other, driven past endurance by the unfair role-reversal that aging forces upon parents and children. I felt sympathy for them both but gladly removed from it all. This was not a situation I would ever confront: I had two sisters, better qualified by geography and temperament to look after our parents (both still in good health) if the need arose, and I had no children. When I was as old and frail as Helen Ralston, assuming I made it that long, there would be no one left to care if I looked after myself properly or not. And unless I had the money to pay for it, there would certainly be no expedition for the elderly me like today's.

Although I thought Helen had every right to do what she wanted with what remained of her life—even if it hastened her death—I felt a terrible sad empathy for Clarissa. I thought we both had guessed the real reason for Helen's determination to visit the little death-island again, and I wondered how we would manage if the old woman simply refused to leave it.

Something like that must have been going through Clarissa's mind when she broke the stalemate with her mother and asked me, "Will I be able to get a signal on my mobile phone out here?"

I shrugged. "You can try. I've got a short-wave radio on board for emergencies."

The tension left her shoulders. "That's good to know. Shall we go?"

There were a few minor hair-raising moments still ahead, helping Helen into the dinghy, but we finally managed to make landfall on Achlan, and I was the only one who got even slightly wet.

"Shall we have our picnic on that big flat rock over there?" asked Clarissa. "It looks like a nice spot."

"We can rest and eat at the shrine," said Helen. "I'm not stopping now." She turned to me. "You can take my picture there, nowhere else."

"Do you remember how to get there? Is it far?" I looked at the thin, blue-veined, old woman's ankles above the sensible sturdy shoes, and recalled Willy Logan's description of the long, slow, torturous descent over rough, rocky ground, leaning heavily on his lover and suffering many stumbles and painful encounters with brambles, nettles, and rabbit holes that he was unable to avoid in his blindness.

"How far can it be?" Helen replied unhelpfully. "Anyway, we'll follow the water-course; that will take us to the source."

I followed the direction of her gaze and realized when I glimpsed the fresh water tumbling over rocks to spill into the bay that I had been hearing its roar, subtly different from the rumble of the waves, ever since we'd landed.

Following the stream might have been sensible, but it wasn't easy. Even so early in spring there was a riot of vegetation to slow our progress, wicked blackberry vines that snatched at our clothing and scored our flesh, roots and unseen rocks and hollows to trip us up. Clarissa and I led fairly sedentary lives and were not as fit as we might have been, but we were still relatively supple and capable of putting on the occasional burst of speed.

Helen, so much older, had fewer reserves. It must have been many years since she had walked for more than ten minutes at a stretch or over anything more taxing than a roughly-pebbled drive. Within minutes, her breathing was sounding tortured, and I knew she must be in pain, pushing herself to her limit. Yet, no matter what we said, she would not consider giving up or turning back. A little rest was all she needed, she said, and then we could go on. And so, every three or four minutes, she would give a gasp and stop walking, her shoulders rising up and down as, for a full minute, she marshaled her resources to continue.

Of course we stayed with her, standing in harsh sunlight or in buzzing, leafy shade, during her frequent rest-stops, and then continuing to creep up the gentle slope of the island, plodding along like weary tortoises.

I recalled Helen Ralston's comment as a young woman that in this island she had seen her death and Willy Logan's conviction that "death" meant something else. But maybe he was wrong. Maybe death was just death, and Helen, now so near to the end of life, had finally come to meet it.

We crept along in silence except for the whine and tortured pant of Helen's breathing and the laughing bubbling rush of the stream, and the background sough of wind and sea. I kept my eyes fixed on the ground, mostly, on the look-out for hazards. The sounds, our unnaturally slow pace, my worries about what was going to happen all combined to affect my brain, and after a while it seemed to me that the earth beneath my feet had become flesh, that I was treading upon a gigantic female body. This was bad enough, but there was something stranger to come, as it seemed I felt the footsteps upon my own, naked, supine body: that I was the land, and it was me. My body began to ache, but it seemed there was nothing to be done. I lost track of time, and my sense of myself as an individual became tenuous.

"Is that it?"

Clarissa's voice cut through the feverish dream or self-hypnosis or whatever it was that had possessed me, and I raised my head with a gasp, like someone who had been swimming for too long underwater, and looked around.

The stream had dwindled into a bubbling rill between two rocks. Nearby I saw a large tumble of stones, partly overgrown by brambles and weeds. Impossible to say now what it might once have been—a tomb, a sheep-fank, or a tumble-down cottage—but clearly they had been piled up deliberately by someone sometime in the past.

"Look at me. Now."

It was Helen's voice, but so different that I thought maybe I'd heard it only in my head. Yet at the same time I knew that she was speaking to me. I looked around and met her eyes. What happened then I can't describe, can barely remember. I think I saw something that I shouldn't have seen. But maybe it was nothing to do with sight, was purely a brain event. I flail around for an explanation, or at least a metaphor. It was like a lightning bolt, fairy-stroke, the touch of the Goddess, death itself, birth.

The next thing I knew, I was lying on the ground, naked beneath the high, cloudy sky. I heard water sounds and the noise of someone weeping.

There was an awful, dull ache in my back. I opened my eyes and sat up slowly, painfully, wondering what had happened. I smelled sweat and blood and sex and crushed vegetation. I remembered looking at Helen, but if that had been seconds ago, or hours, or even longer, I had no idea. The other two women were gone. I was alone with a man—a naked man huddled a few feet away from me, beside the cairn he'd named a shrine, and weeping. I recognized him as Willy Logan.

Then I understood who I was.

I was Helen Ralston.

NOW, MORE than a year later, I am still Helen, as I will be, I suppose, until I die.

I avoid mirrors. It gives me a sickening, horrific jolt to see those alien, deep-set eyes glaring back at me out of another woman's face, even if the terror I feel is reflected in hers.

Of course I keep what I know to myself—I certainly have no desire to be locked up in an early twentieth century loony bin—and, as time goes by, it has become somewhat easier. Memories of my other life and of that other world that I suppose to be the future are growing dimmer, harder to recall and to believe. That's why I decided to write this, before it is forever too late. The words in this book, which I intend to keep safe, will ensure that what happened once doesn't have to go on happening into an infinity of futures— unless I want it to. I will show it to myself when the time is right, seventy-three years from now.

The feeling of dislocation, of alienation and fear, which I had at first, has eased with the passage of time. The strangeness has faded like my impossible, disturbing memories, and the sense of being embarked upon a great adventure—a new life!—has become more powerful. After all, this is not such a bad time or place to be young and alive.

—Helen Elizabeth Ralston
Paris
22 September 1930

THE INTERVIEW—my one and only interview with Helen—had not gone exactly as she described. For one thing, she'd been more disabled by her stroke than the story indicated, and the conversation between us had been painfully repetitious, slow and circular. She did mention a few famous names, people she had known in Paris and London in the 1930s, but her anecdotes had a way of petering out rather than coming to a point, and one story would frequently blend into another, so that an incident that took place in pre-war Paris would segue abruptly into something that had happened to her in post-war London. I felt sorry for her and rather frustrated as I realized I was unlikely to get much first-hand information from her for my book.

After about an hour, Clarissa took her mother upstairs to bed. When she came back down, she gave me the notebook.

"Mum wants you to have this," she said. "She wants you to read it."

I took the old, hard-bound notebook with a feeling of great privilege and excitement. "What is it? Did she say?"

"She said it has the deepest, most important truth about her life."

"Wow."

We smiled at each other—the charge of sympathetic, affectionate sympathy between us was very real—and she invited me to stay and have a bite to eat. We spent maybe an hour over coffee and cake, talking, getting to know each other. I left, then, and after a detour to do some shopping at Braehead, drove home.

I remember the details of my arrival home—putting away the groceries, looking through the mail, heating up a Marks and Spencer Indian meal and then eating it while listening to "Front Row" on Radio 4—as if they were incidents from a lost Eden of innocence. Afterwards, I brewed a pot of herbal tea and took it upstairs to my office. There, at my desk, I pushed the keyboard aside, set Helen Ralston's book where it had been and pulled the reading light forward and angled it down to cast a strong cone of light directly onto the page. I began to read and fell into the abyss.

It was after midnight when I finished reading, my neck and spine aching from the tense crouch I'd maintained for hours at my desk as I struggled to decipher her cramped, narrow writing. I was trembling with exhaustion, terror, and bewilderment.

How was this possible? Could her story be true?

If it wasn't, how did she know so much about me? How was she able to write in my voice, including so many accurate details about my life and everything that had happened starting with the chain of events that had caused me to decide to write a biography of Helen Ralston up to our first meeting?

I didn't sleep that night.

At eight o'clock the next morning, so blank, cold, and numb that I could have said I was feeling nothing at all, I telephoned Clarissa Breen and asked to speak to Helen.

In a voice that wavered slightly, she told me her mother was dead.

"It happened not long after you left. Or maybe...maybe before." She took a deep breath. "She was sleeping when I left her to come downstairs to you. Normally, she'll sleep for about two hours. At lunchtime, I went upstairs to check on her. As soon as I went into her bedroom I knew. She was gone."

All my questions seemed suddenly insignificant, and the terror that had gripped me loosed its hold. I rushed to sympathize, uttering all the usual, insufficient phrases of sorrow and respect.

"Thank you. I was going to call you, later today. I wanted to thank you—for coming when you did and making Mum's last day so special. She was happy, you know, really thrilled to be meeting you. Not just because of the biography—of course it was great for her to know she hadn't been forgotten—but because it was *you*. She loved your work, you know. She'd been reading your stories since you were first published—she always felt there was a special connection between you."

I shivered convulsively and gripped the phone hard. "Did she *say* that?"

"Oh—it was obvious how she felt. Didn't I tell you, that's why I read that book of yours, because you were obviously so important to her. Anyway, I wanted you to know how much your coming meant to her. It was the first time I'd seen her happy and excited in—well, the last seven months were very hard for her. Since the stroke, and having to leave London, no longer able to live on her own. I—I really thought this was going to be the start of a new phase for her, I can't quite—I'm sorry..." she stumbled, then recovered herself. "I can't quite believe she's gone. But it was the best way, to go like that, suddenly and all at once, it's what she wanted—she hated the idea of another, even more crippling, stroke—so did I—of dwindling away in a hospital bed, dying by inches."

We talked for a few more minutes. Clarissa had a lot to do; she promised she'd let me know about the funeral.

I went to Glasgow for it the following week and took the notebook and the painting to give back. I found my chance after the cremation when we few mourners—most of them Clarissa's own friends and extended family—gathered in her house to eat the traditional cold food. I took the notebook out of my bag, but she shook her head and told me it was mine.

"Mum wanted you to have it. No, I mean it; she couldn't have been more clear about her wishes; she left instructions in her will. In fact, not just the notebook, but a painting as well. It's called *My Death*, she said it's a watercolor, but I've never seen it—I'm sure Mum didn't keep any of her early works, she never mentioned it before, and in the will she didn't explain where it was or anything."

I launched into a rushed, stumbling explanation of how I'd come into possession of *My Death* until she stopped me with a hand on my shoulder. "That's all right. That's fine. I'm glad you've got it. It was what she wanted."

"I've got it in the car—I was going to give it back to you—"

"No, you must keep it."

"Well—would you like to see it? Just before I go. It's in the car."

She nodded slowly. "Yes. Yes I would. Thank you. I know Mum was an artist before she was a writer, but I've never seen anything she painted."

We left the house and walked down to the street where my car was parked. My heart began to pound unpleasantly as I took the wrapped parcel out of the boot, and I wondered if I should try to warn her, to prepare her in some way. But the words would not come, and so I unwrapped it in silence and laid it down, face up, inside the open boot of the car, and we looked down upon *My Death* in silence.

A watercolor landscape in tones of blue and brown and grey and green and pink, a rocky island in the sea. Tears blurred my vision and I looked away in time to see Clarissa dash her hand across her eyes and give a soft, shuddering sigh.

She turned away, and I put my arms around her.

"Thank you," she murmured, returning my hug.

I kissed her cheek. "Let's stay in touch."

OTHER NEW YORK REVIEW CLASSICS

For a complete list of titles, visit www.nyrb.com.